Bright Sari in a Darkened Street

Ian M. Emberson

2QT
PUBLISHING

First Edition published 2018 by
2QT Limited (Publishing)
Settle, North Yorkshire BD24 9RH United Kingdom

Cover Design by Charlotte Mouncey
Cover image based on Photo by Saksham Gangwar on Unsplash.com

Printed in Great Britain by Lightning Source UK Ltd

A CIP catalogue record for this book is available from the British Library
ISBN 978-1-912014-16-3

PRELUDE

Holmefield, 2006

The bright sari, purple, set against the dull morning street. That was what drew Miles' attention. He swept his hands through his already greying hair and looked at the Indian girl intently. If only she would stay still then he could paint her. Perhaps he should go across and ask her to stand there. But no. That would be an intrusion. She was obviously on her way somewhere special to be wearing that beautiful sari at mid-morning, actually trailing the tail of it over the dirty pavement of grey Yorkshire millstone as she moved.

Still, there were plenty of other things to put in the picture. There was plenty of life. Those children playing, for example: three little Sikh boys with guttees on their heads, a tiny Hindu girl with red kurta and salwar, and two little white boys – or off-white – with dust and grime on their faces. And beyond them the cobbled street, terraced houses, mill chimneys (yes – a few still left from the great demolition craze of long ago back in the 1980s) and the moors. The great sweep of the Pennines, dull and grey in the morning heat.

But that girl in the purple sari – what a pity she hadn't lingered. With her in the foreground the picture would have symbolised something special, those intense years back in his late teens and early twenties. Miles had known much since then, including some modest success as an artist. Happiness too, at least recently. But nothing as intense as those years. That was impossible.

It had been the time of his awakening as an artist. Everything had seemed so fresh then, so very fresh. It was all these things. But then it was Kavita. Yes. Basically it was Kavita.

Part One

ONE

Kavita. Right, where do we begin? But no. We don't begin with Kavita. She will come in soon enough. We begin with Miles. Miles as he was then at seventeen, well-nigh twenty years ago.

*

It was early summer, May 1986. The evening art class was meeting in its studio on the edge of Holmefield, a moderately sized, industrial town in a valley in the west of Yorkshire. Not far off were the mills, factories and office blocks but here, close to the river, with a bird-cherry in blossom beyond the window and a blackbird singing its evening call of love or hate, one could almost imagine oneself to be far off in the countryside

It was a small class – only seven – and they were sitting in a rough semi-circle, easels, boards and paints at the ready, waiting for the model to take up her pose. The young model, meantime, stood to one side in her red dressing gown. The elderly art teacher, Mrs Crowther, waggled her thin lips and hooked nose as she discussed with her what pose to use and for how long. Beauty and the Beast flashed momentarily through Miles' mind.

Miles was the youngest of the group. He sat there resting his long pale face on his right hand, whilst with his left he pushed back his unruly hair – dark, with the merest hint of auburn. He felt shy, self-conscious. It was his first visit to the class and he had never seen a woman naked before; the time he pushed open the bathroom door, forgetting his aunt was having a bath, didn't really count. He couldn't quite believe that this nameless girl was going to undress. But yes, there she was taking off that red dressing gown and settling into her pose on the Windsor chair, her body turned somewhat, right arm flung behind, right breast silhouetted against the chair back. It was all so unemotional, matter-of-fact; she could have been a vase of flowers or a bowl of fruit.

'Right, this is the pose for the next hour,' Mrs Crowther announced.

The members of the class reacted in their respective ways: the neatly-bearded young man beside Miles seemed far more interested in sharpening his pencils than in the model, whilst a Rubenesque female opposite attacked her paper vigorously with a charcoal stump as if fearing the model would suddenly assume invisibility. But Miles just looked – looked – nothing more. And there she was, this girl without a name but with so much beauty. Just out of girlhood into womanhood, early twenties presumably; hair lightish brown (lovely, that contrast of the curving shoulder and the light brown hair); eyes almost violet; body – the merest suggestion of an overall tan but faint, very faint. And then the light from the window made all the difference: a warm May evening light touching the highlights on the left upper arm and the right knee, spreading soft, deep, graduated shadows below the right thigh and between the breasts.

But this was no use – he was supposed to be drawing. Yet when he glanced down at the paper he realised that in a strange sort of way he had already started for, whilst he had been looking, his pencil had subconsciously meandered over the paper. Pencil, rubber and pad – that was all Miles had brought with him; he didn't want to be too ambitious to begin with. And it was in this dreamy way that Miles continued. He didn't bother with holding his pencil at arm's length and taking proportions, nothing like that. He just let the lines form faintly and randomly whilst he looked at the girl.

And yes, when he eventually glanced down at the paper something was emerging. Like a hillside seen through the clearing morning mist, the shoulder and upper arm were assuming shape through the tangle of pallid lines. He had never before been so thrilled by his own creativity. God, how dull the art class at his sixth-form college seemed by contrast.

Mrs Crowther tiptoed her way round the room like a cautious cat ready to spring. She paused beside each student, looked for a while and then made comments, long or short as appropriate. She came to Miles and stood there for some while. Miles paused in his work, fearing he would make some blunder whilst she was watching him. But all she said was 'um' and passed on. What did that 'um' mean? Very good? Very bad? Or just too indifferent to comment on?

*

After the class was over, Miles packed his drawing board under his arm and walked back to his home village of Tostenland where his stepfather was vicar. It was three miles but he always enjoyed the walk, especially on that evening when the loveliness of the evening sunlight seemed to accentuate the mood engendered by drawing that nameless girl. Why, even the mills appeared somehow noble as the rays flooded their newly cleaned sandstone walls. They'd been worth cleaning now that Holmefield was smokeless. And further on up the valley side, the poking bluebells relieved the erstwhile winter-russet of woodland and the chestnuts were greening up against the May-time sky.

The road rounded a hilltop and down in the dip beyond lay Tostenland.

TWO

Tostenland; you could see it for miles around if you knew where to look. That long dip in the hills and, at its centre, the spire of the Victorian-Gothic church spiking up at the sky. Beyond lay the empty moors and below was the Fielden Valley, with a long straggle of mills along its floor.

But Tostenland itself didn't quite have the harshness of its surroundings. Why was that? Maybe because not all the field divisions were stone walls; in places there were hawthorn hedges, now flooded with small white flowers. Or perhaps it was the lush woodland, hollies and oaks mostly, which skirted the contours of the hills on either side.

Miles felt rather shy walking into the village that evening with his art pad tucked under his arm. The first person he met was Nick the tractor driver, clutching a bag of spanners and other tools.

'T'owd bugger's broken dahn in't Seat Field. Would yer believe it? Ah tell thi it's put t'mockers on all mi plans fer t'evening's work.'

'Oh dear.'

'Yeah. What's that ye've got under yer arm?'

'Art book.'

'Err.'

To Miles' relief the conversation went no further. But then at the bend of the road he met Clare on her skewbald pony, Tara. Even she made him feel strange, which was silly; after all, they had played together enough in childhood. But there was something special about Clare, something he normally took for granted but which struck him now as she rode towards him.

Or perhaps it was just that she suddenly looked so beautiful, so grown up too, with her breasts pressed against her white blouse and her fair hair tumbling below her black riding cap. Yes: it was since she had left school and started part time on the farm next door to her home that she seemed suddenly to have ceased being a girl. Somehow she was a woman now. Hard to believe that Clare was really only a few months older than he was.

'Been to art class?' she shouted from about twenty yards away. Clare was keen on art.

'Yes.'

'I'll see you later.'

And with that, Clare lightly jerked her heels into Tara's flanks and Miles felt the air flush by as the pony broke into a gallop along the dry, springy verge.

After the sensual beauty of the spring evening, the austere millstone walls of the vicarage seemed almost prison-like. The angelic boy who formed a sort of gargoyle on the keystone appeared to smirk at Miles with a half-satanic leer. Strange that Miles hadn't noticed that look before. After all, the place had been his home for five years now, ever since his widowed mother had married the vicar, although Miles had lived in the village all his life. Those earlier years had been spent at Blackroyd, an isolated stone-built house, now derelict, which lay halfway between Clare's place and The Bare-Knuckle

Boys, a pub at which Miles' father had well-nigh drank himself to death.

Miles walked into the cool hallway. The study door was shut and he knew that his stepfather would be inside preparing his Sunday sermon. He found his mother in the living room sitting by the window knitting, the rays of a strong sunset just touching on her greying hair.

She laid the knitting down as he came in. 'Only three more rows and I'll have the sleeve finished.'

'What's it for?'

'A pullover for the home-made stall at the church summer bazaar.'

'Oh.'

'Yes, I told you. You are going to look after a stall with Sally, aren't you?'

'Yes, of course.' Miles wondered why he felt so little enthusiasm. Only a few days ago he had been quite looking forward to helping Sally on the stall.

'Well, what have you been drawing?' Miles picked up the art book and opened it. 'What's that?' his mother asked.

'A woman.'

'Yes, I can see it's a woman but she hasn't any clothes on.'

'That's right.'

'But I thought it was an art class you were going to.'

'It is – life drawing.'

'I don't think you should be doing things like this.'

'Why not? All the great artists painted the nude body – Rubens and Michelangelo and...'

'That was quite different. They were famous artists.'

Miles shrugged and didn't reply. In a way he was less annoyed than he might have expected by his mother's narrow-mindedness. It was really rather funny. But he decided to retreat for a bit so he picked up his art book and went to his room.

The view from Miles' bedroom looked right across the Fielden Valley to the slow curves of the Pennines. What a sunset it was tonight – beautiful yet somehow sinister. Most of the sky was cloudless but there, just above where the sun was poised on the moorland's edge, was an army of close-packed clouds. The sun, as it cut itself in two on the horizon, sent rays of vivid red across this cloudscape – a bloodstain, a slowly seeping bloodstain.

THREE

Miles looked for a long time at the squashed tube of toothpaste. This was the subject for today's session at Longworth Sixth-Form College – a squashed tube. Somewhere he remembered he had read that nothing was so trivial or so ugly that it might not be the subject matter for art. He tried very hard to convince himself of this philosophy as he picked up his pencil.

In about a quarter of an hour Miles had drawn the squashed tube. Mr Duggan the art master shuffled round the room, brushing his ancient suit against the rows of stuffed birds and the pupils' desks. He paused beside Miles. 'Um,' he said, just like Mrs Crowther. Miles was beginning to think that was only word of criticism that would ever be bestowed upon his work. But then he added, 'Too small,' with a bitter hiss in his voice.

'Too small'? What did he mean: 'too small'? Miles knew a bit of art history; Van Dyck could paint a horse life size and Bewick engrave one half an inch high but they were both good horses. But there was still plenty of time in hand so Miles thought he might as well do another one – even if it was only the first one on a bigger scale.

Whilst he did the second drawing, his attention wandered to his fellow pupils. Spinks was drawing a cock and balls on the back of his paper; Fenwick was manufacturing paper pellets and flicking them at Squires; Burton had found a print of the Mona Lisa and was turning it into a paper aeroplane. Only Vora, the Indian boy, seemed to be doing what he was supposed to be doing, his nose to the board and his pencil moving feverishly.

Miles glanced at his drawing. It wasn't very good but that was certainly not for lack of diligence.

*

After college, Miles went straight to the art section of the public library. This had been his secret consolation for some while, ever since he had happened on it by accident when returning a theology book for his stepfather. All the old friends were there: Leonardo; Rembrandt; Turner; Constable; Picasso, etc. He had borrowed them all before, usually just overnight, looking at the pictures and skimming the text. But today there was someone he didn't remember seeing before: Chagall.

Miles opened the big book at random. In front of him was a picture, a beautiful chaos of blues and purples, reds and greens. Rather slowly his mind reorganised this brilliance into shapes, objects. Most vivid of all, like a blue fragment of mother-of-pearl, was the Eiffel Tower. In front, a newly-wed couple (he purple, she white) were buoyed aloft by a gigantic chicken – not a real chicken but a child's stuffed toy. All around hung confused images: angels, candlesticks, a violin, a bull. And all this was curdled and mixed, as if the ebullience of a child's unfettered mind was still wildly present in a world of passionate adulthood.

Miles was just about to take the book to be stamped when he noticed that Mr Duggan was standing at the counter. Miles had no wish to meet him so he went round to the other side of the shelving and pretended to look at some more books. Beside him stood two rather artistic-looking men; one was tall, broad shouldered and auburn-bearded, the other small and sepia brown. They too were looking at Mr Duggan.

'Good God! Duggan's over there,' said the big man. 'Perhaps he's come to borrow *Teach Yourself Painting* – it's time he learnt. Submitted ten canvasses to the Holmefield Art Exhibition last year. Nine were rejects and the tenth only got through out of kindness. Doesn't even know how to draw. They say he teaches at Longworth – God help the pupils.'

Miles sniggered to himself as he took the Chagall book to the counter. As he came down the library steps he could see Mr Duggan walking past the Town Hall.

'You squashed tube,' Miles muttered

*

When he got home, he tucked the Chagall under his arm and went for a walk. He followed the snaking twists of Marsh Hall Lane and climbed the hillside above Heights Farm as far as the stile on the first stone wall. There he stopped and, sitting on one of the flatter stones, he opened the book and looked through the pictures.

As before, it was the sheer brilliance of the colours that struck him: the blues, the reds, the greens, the yellows – but above all the blues. Yet they were the same colours that all artists used so what was different? Somehow this artist had made them different – so brilliant, so exciting. Then there were the recurring themes: the eternal cockerel forever crowing in some corner of the canvas; the strange fish rowing their way with human hands across the painted air; the lovers cavorting in a whirl of ecstasy.

When he eventually put down the book, Miles had a curious feeling that the village had suddenly changed. The church, the trees, the little fields of many colours, all seemed to be leaping in his imagination like the streaming notes of a brilliant toccata, rivalling one another to express what they were, what they meant, what they felt. Something from a childhood fantasy seemed to be joined for a moment to the precision of adulthood. Briefly Miles seemed to see, plain and naked, the meaning of expression, of art – almost of life itself.

Then abruptly everything went back to its normal self: the church was just a church, the trees were trees, the fields were fields.

FOUR

That moment, almost like a vision, seemed to set something alight in Miles. From then on he was always drawing and painting. It was not just the countryside that excited him; the streets of Holmefield suddenly appeared full of interest too.

On sunny afternoons he put up his easel on the edge of one of the cobbled side streets. Perhaps a group of West Indian boys would be playing football, their tricolour Rasta hats pressed tight on their frizzy hair. Or the Hindu children would hold a mock battle, scarlet kurtas and salwars flying as they ran. Whatever was happening Miles put it in the picture; he wanted life, the human element.

But sometimes the human element became a bit much as the kids gathered round his easel.

'Look – an artist!'

'Don't think much to that.'

'Who d'you think you are – Picasso?'

But even that didn't put him off.

Then there were the buildings. Those two big, round tunnel vents up at Springwood always made Miles think of the twin funnels of a half-submerged liner, as if it had sunk amid the flotsam and jetsam of little houses. Nearby, like three great rocks towering from the sea, stood the Co-op, the Town Hall and the library, their cliffs and crevasses seagulled with the evening clatter of starlings.

Then there were the mills lower down the valley, which Miles painted with feverish haste as if fearing they would all be knocked down before he could finish. Sometimes he drew them half-demolished, the bulldozers charging around like angry tigers; once he watched a great, grey, mill chimney, which had darkly fingered the sky for a hundred years, crash down into a chaos of mud and debris.

But neither did he forget the countryside – its harvest was also endless. Yes, there was subject matter there for a lifetime, for many lifetimes. Even his home village held enough: the Victorian-Gothic Church; the crumbling moss-grown walls; the spinneys of beech and ash; the haphazardly built farm buildings; the many-windowed weavers' cottages.

There was all this – and the changing seasons forever playing their variations on it – whilst higher up the landscape became more treeless until it gave way to the open moors where there was nothing but tough grass, heather, bilberry, gurgling streams, soft peat hags, grouse, skylarks and curlews.

There was one thing he didn't paint any more or at least not for a long, long time: the female nude. Miles could be very conformist. He hadn't forgotten the model's soft beauty and his wish to capture it in a work of art but his mother's implied disapproval had a curiously deadening effect. It wasn't for many years that his pencil once again traced the sinuous lines of a woman's body.

FIVE

That summer seemed to have made up its mind to be warm, with the morning sun rising clear above the misting valleys each day: regular, predictable. It was on one such morning that Miles caught the bus down into Holmefield. The countryside didn't draw him today – why? He wasn't sure. He knew he just wanted to sketch in the city – nothing ambitious, just sketches, nothing more – so all he had was a pencil and a very small pad.

Miles sat down on the edge of the piazza, a small grassy area between the shoe-box shape of the library and a semi-circle of shops. Being Saturday, there were few people around as yet, just some early-morning shoppers buying sweets and newspapers at a kiosk. He began to sketch anything – the buildings, the early-leafing trees, the pigeons cooing optimistically at his feet. Then something started happening: four workmen in blue overalls appeared and began assembling stands, trestle tables and chairs on the grass in front of him. Miles asked one of them what was happening.

'Bloody National Arts Day – as if I hadn't worked hard enough this week already. I like me ale on a Friday night and a good sleep in on't Saturday. 'Stead of which we've got to put up all these 'ere stalls. Culture, music, art, dancing – all that crap.'

Miles smiled and made a hasty sketch of the man pressing his bulging stomach against the tables as he carried them across the grass. Then he made some other sketches: the little fat lady soaking oasis at the flower stall, and the bearded secretary of the Arts Council flapping around in an incompetent tizz, trying to organise everyone.

The stalls were soon assembled and innumerable helpers began decorating them with their appropriate wares – books, records and paintings. A microphone appeared and was tested. The event was obviously about to be opened.

A man approached and began speaking. Miles recognised him as the person who had made the disparaging remarks about Mr Duggan in the library. Miles asked the lady at the flower-arranging stall who he was.

'Why, that's Randal Bramley. He's well-known. Painter – surely you've heard of him.'

Miles had, and he knew of Randal's big reputation. Interested, he drew nearer. Only half-listening to the speech, he started to draw the speaker: the big woollen pullover pulled down over the slight spread of early middle-age; the auburn and grey beard and eyebrows that looked like overseas colonies of the pullover; the broad chest, strong arms and the one-size-too-big trousers.

The speech ended. A small flutter of applause came from the few people who had bothered to listen. Then a moment of panic: Miles realised that Randal was about to walk past him. Should he pretend to be doing something else? But no – he carried on drawing some vague diagonal lines as a background to the sketch.

'Well, what have you made of me then young man?'

Miles shyly held up the sketch book.

'Not bad – not bad. But I don't think my eyebrows are quite that bushy. You're turning me into an Old English Sheepdog.'

They talked for some while, Randal looking through the rest of Miles' sketchbook and taking a real interest in his work. Miles was flattered; he had never had an eminent artist's opinion before. The upshot was that Randal persuaded him to join the local art society and Miles, who had a way of taking advice very literally, went at once across to their stall for an enrolment form. Then he stood for a while looking at the paintings and the posters for forthcoming events.

While he was thus engaged, he heard a soft twanging sound close by and looked up. A stage had been erected in the centre of the piazza and at one corner an Indian sat on a cushion dressed in soft white baggy trousers. In front of him were three small drums. At the other corner, a tall bearded gentleman held an instrument a bit like a guitar but with a large circular sounding-board near its base. It was this that Miles had heard make the twanging sound; for some while it carried on with a rather nondescript tuning up.

Suddenly a young Hindu girl leapt onto the stage and began dancing – dark, agile, beautiful. Her kurta was purple and covered in little bells, which rang as she leapt; her arms, long and slim, rattled with gold bracelets; her deep brown eyes flashed like a weasel's. She was soft and lamb-like and yet somehow ferocious as well, like a tigress – a springing tigress.

Miles wondered at her dancing. What did it mean? He was sure it meant something. And then she started moving very strangely. Ripples seemed to rush all through her body and her arms and fingers twisted like worms writhing in agony. She seemed to go into a sort of frenzy then suddenly she fell on the floor, apparently dead.

Another girl came on the stage, dressed in yellow and green. She wandered round and round the stage making gestures as if asking questions. Then she came across the body. For a moment she made the movements of somebody drinking then knelt down, touched the body with concern, moved off, stooped down, returned, rubbed a spot on the forearm. The body slowly revived, stood up, came back to life. The two dancers linked arms and did a joyful dance together.

That was the end of this dance. Afterwards two grotesque figures came on dressed as Indian gods but Miles wasn't interested. His eyes followed the young girl in purple as she left the stage. She nodded and smiled at a young Indian boy and seemed to be about to go up to him. But an older man, thirtyish and neatly dressed, bore down on her and held her in conversation.

Miles looked again at the boy she had nodded to and realised it was Kamlesh Vora from Longworth. Miles went across to him. 'You know that girl?'

'She's my sister.'

'She is very beautiful.'

'She is my sister,' Kamlesh repeated.

'Can you introduce me?' Miles, like most very shy people, suffered from spasms of impulsive self-confidence. 'Can you introduce me?' he repeated, glancing towards the girl and noticing she was still talking to the older man but half-turned away as if about to leave.

'Yes – yes. She may be glad of an excuse to throw off Dr Vyas. But what shall I say?'

'That I admire her dancing.'

Kamlesh shrugged and walked towards his sister, breaking in on her conversation. The doctor shuffled uneasily, muttered something inaudible and moved away while the girl gave a sort of silent giggle and turned her eyes towards Miles.

'Kavita, this is Miles, my school friend. He is very interested in your dancing.'

The weasel eyes darted at him, gently mischievous. 'Oh – so you liked my snake-charmer act? Did it charm you?'

'Yes, yes – but I thought you were portraying the snake.'

'No, the snake charmer imitates the snake in order to charm him. Listen, let me tell you the story.' As she said this, she touched the back of his hand with her fingers for a moment. She smiled and the dimples at the base of her cheeks puckered. 'You see, it is like this. The snake charmer is charming the snake. He uses all his arts but it is a new and very dangerous snake. Suddenly it strikes. The poison goes into a wound in the left forearm – here. He falls insensible. Then the snake-charmer's wife wonders why he is late – that is my sister Aditi.' She pointed to the girl in yellow and green. 'She sets off to search for him. Many people she asks, "Have you seen my husband?" and she describes him: "He is tall and very black, and with a great big belly with too much drinking – that is my husband…"'

'But how could a man like that writhe and twist like a snake. How on earth could a girl like you portray him?'

'Yes, it is funny. I hadn't thought of that – but you must believe it.' Kavita took his hand again. 'Though it is only a story. And so she comes to her husband. At first she thinks he is just drunk as usual but then she sees the horrible wound on his forearm. She gathers medicinal herbs, puts them on it and slowly he recovers. Then she is very happy for she loves her husband, even although he is a drunkard. And then they dance a happy dance together.'

'Have you done these dances for a long time?'

'Since I was a tiny little girl – so high – in Bombay.'

'How long have you been here?'

'Ten years but some things still seem strange in a way.'

'Such as?'

'Well, that girl over there showing so much bare leg – and those two kissing away… But – well – one gets used to everything eventually.' She giggled.

'How old are you?'

'Seventeen. You ask too many questions.'

'I'm sorry.'

'Oh, don't misunderstand. I meant no offence. My brother Kamlesh is a friend of yours then?'

'We're at Longworth together.'

'I'm at sixth-form college too – Springwood.' Again she giggled slightly nervously and touched the back of his hand. She added, 'Come round to our house sometime – as a friend of the family, you know. People are always dropping in. It's by Vora's General Stores in Wesley Street – number sixteen.'

'Yes, thanks. Goodbye Ka...'

'Kavita. It means poetry. You see – I am a poem.'

'Kavita.'

'Yes. You pronounce it well. Goodbye, Miles – I have a better memory.'

SIX

Miles had that image of the Indian girl focused in his mind: the writhing, beautiful ugliness of the snake movements; the soft exotic voice (was there just a hint of a Yorkshire accent?) and the lovely dimples below her cheeks, which puckered as she smiled. And with this image went a certain mood. For several days he felt a sense of calmness, serenity of purpose. Yes, a state of mind he wanted to preserve.

Therefore it was with no great pleasure that he learned on an evening a few days later that his stepfather wished to see him in his study. He had no idea what it was about but he went down the gloomy corridor with a feeling of unease.

His stepfather sat beyond the wide, green-topped desk. He was a handsome man even now he was in his mid-fifties. Miles looked at the haughty nose and strangely sensual mouth, the clear but ruddy skin, incredibly white hair and penetrating blue eyes. His stepfather suddenly made him think of an overgrown cherub.

The blue eyes darted a look of unintended impatience. 'Miles, I've been feeling for some while that we ought to have a chat about – about your future.'

'Yes.'

The vicar seemed disconcerted by the brevity of the reply. He picked up an elastic band from the desk and fiddled with it for some while. 'I mean your career.'

Miles answer this time was merely a nod.

'I've – that is your mother and I – have been thinking that one of the professions might suit you. The legal profession, for example. My brother was a solicitor, as I've told you, and my uncle a judge. Now what I—'

'I'm going to be an artist.'

'An artist. Yes, as a hobby of course. Every retired doctor and fishmonger paints pretty pictures of Castle Hill nowadays, it seems. But what I want to discuss is your profession – how you are going to earn your living.'

'I've already said.'

'Now, now – really, let's be practical. I mean, in the first place a man needs a steady income and in the second – what is art nowadays? The old artists, the great ones, they've been made obsolete by the camera. So what's left? You either do these nondescript abstract daubs, which any intelligent chimpanzee could equal, or you prostitute your talents to the soap companies and tobacco manufacturers. So think of something else – the late twentieth century doesn't need artists.'

Various angry answers sprang to Miles' mind but he supressed them. Instead he just sat there for a while in silence. He looked beyond his stepfather to the window and then a bit to the left where a print of a Leonardo Madonna hung on the wall. It seemed to be saying something to him, divulging some mystery that no photo could ever divulge. The picture led his thoughts to religion, to his stepfather and his aims in life. An argument formed. 'You were once like me, weren't you? Making this sort of decision?'

The vicar blushed. 'My dear boy, it's your life we're talking about not mine. What decisions I made for good or ill – well, they're in the past, more summers back than I care to remember.'

'Yes,' Miles continued, sensing an advantage, 'and you chose religion. And you've continued devoting yourself to it all these years, despite the tiny congregations.'

The vicar nodded. Was this a compliment or an insult? He wasn't sure.

'Alright. Well, that's the way I feel about art. It's the thing I want to devote my life to whatever the consequences.'

His stepfather looked across the green-topped desk at him like one who sees an innocent pawn pushed forward to enact a deadly checkmate. Then abruptly the look of seriousness left his face. He laughed – actually laughed. 'Oh well, I always say I admire a man who knows his own mind.' He placed his palms downward on the desk and tapped it twice with his fingers in unison. Miles knew the gesture. It meant the matter was over.

With a parting glance at the Leonardo Madonna, he left the room.

SEVEN

Yes, that image of the Indian girl was still with him. But what to do about it? Of course he must get to know her. But how? What on earth could he do to get to know her better? Admittedly she'd invited him round to her home; what more could he want? No – that would be awful, so formal. He was far too shy for that. Yet if he rejected that approach, what else was there? A chance encounter? That would be too lucky to hope for.

Even supposing he met her – what then? Miles had heard stories of all sorts of restrictions being put on Indian girls. Perhaps she wouldn't even like him, though she had seemed nice enough at that first meeting. Even if she did, there would probably be numerous complications.

Yet despite all that, he thought of her – thought of her intently. He repeated her name 'Kavita, Kavita', remembered just how she had said, 'You see – I am a poem.' How she had smiled, how she had touched his hand.

Miles was thinking about all this one evening in July as he walked out of the village through the late sunlight, his paints and sketch pad under his arm. He had recently started to paint in acrylics; the new medium thrilled him and he wanted to get as much experience as possible.

He came to the cricket pitch. A game was in progress, the players' whites edged by the warm light against the green fields beyond. Clare was sitting on a wall nearby, her long fair hair stretched down her blue dress.

'You do look beautiful. Can I paint you?' he asked.

'Why not? I don't mind at all. I'll try to keep still.'

Miles laid out his paints and put his drawing board across his knees.

'I'm at a loose end tonight,' Clare continued. 'Normally I go riding with my sister Sheila on a Tuesday but she's gone out with her Indian boyfriend to a—'

'Her Indian boyfriend?'

'Well – sort of. Platonic, I imagine. Sheila's terribly cautious about these things. I reckon she's heading for old maidhood. Anyway, whatever it is, she's met this chap through her social work and they're out together this evening.'

'Do your parents and his parents allow it?'

'Our parents don't seem to mind – Mother, that is. Father never says anything anyway so I don't know about his side of it. I gather that a lot of Hindus think it's all right for their sons to go out with white girls but not for their daughters to do the same with white boys.'

'Why's that?'

'I don't know – the usual double standard, I suppose. Why are you so interested?'

'I know an Indian girl. That is, I've met her once.'

'And you like her? You want to go out with her but you're afraid of the difficulties?'

'That's right. How did you guess?'

'I've got secret powers. But come on – you're supposed to be doing a painting.'

Miles had almost forgotten. Roused, he squirted some ultramarine blue – a lovely vivid speck of it – onto his palette then mixed in some white. He looked at the sky, still light and with no suggestion of dusk, and began laying on the colour as a broad wash.

'Tell me about this girl,' Clare suddenly said. 'Describe her to me.'

'Her name is Kavita.'

'That tells me a lot. What does she look like?'

'She's a dancer. Very delicate build, perhaps as tall as you – no, not quite. Her eyes are dark and vivid. They dance as well. She wears purple – at least she did the day I saw her – with little bells which tinkle as she dances.'

'She sounds lovely. I should like to meet her. But how do you intend to get to know her better?'

'I don't know.'

'Haven't you got some link with her – some connection?'

'I know her brother.'

'Well, you must work on that.'

'Yes. And she did give me an invitation to her house— "Come round as a friend of the family," she said – something like that.'

'So what are you waiting for?'

'I'm too shy.'

'Too shy?'

'Yes. I mean, just to go round to her house like that without anything more being said...'

'Don't be silly. Just go. Go on. "Faint heart never won fair lady," you know. That's a quote from *Iolanthe* by the way. Did you know I'm in the chorus? Nat's playing Stephan. It's odd having a boyfriend who's a fairy below the waist.'

'You've been going out with him long enough,' Miles said – as if that made the situation normal.

'Yes – neither of us ever seemed to want anyone else,' Clare murmured, half to herself. Then, turning to Miles: 'By the way, are you still going to that art class?'

'What? Oh, you mean the life drawing.'

'Yes. I saw you once with your art pad when I was riding Tara.'

'Oh no. My mother didn't approve so I stopped it.'

'You stopped it? You are easily put off. I thought youth was the time for rebelling, not for bowing to one's parents' most stupid taboos. I rebel against everything. Anyway, that's enough chat. You get on with the painting now.'

The conversation had distracted Miles from the picture. He looked down at the paper and back at Clare. She didn't look much of a rebel – quite the reverse. It was only her taste in clothes that was strange: the long sixties'-style dress she was wearing. Perhaps once it might have been a symbol. Now it was merely eccentric – or individualistic.

But soon Miles forgot everything except the wish to capture Clare on his sheet of paper. The blues, the whites, the greens, were squeezed onto the palette and mixed and the quick-drying acrylics enabled him to finish the picture in an hour, with Clare staying remarkably still. When it was completed and he looked down at the paper, he felt fairly satisfied but when he looked back at Clare and the quiet summer landscape beyond, for a moment he felt that all art was futile. Could it ever compete with nature? Should it? And he looked sadly from the blobbed effects on the paper to the exquisite glossy folds of Clare's hair.

'Can I move now?'

'Yes – yes.'

'Let's look.' She gazed at the picture for some while. 'Not bad.'

'Oh well, that's alright. Kamlesh – Kavita's brother – says that when a Yorkshire person says "not bad", that's the equivalent of anyone else saying "fantastic".'

'Never mind what the brother says, you concentrate on the sister. Get round to the house. I will expect a progress report next time we meet.'

She squeezed his hand and was gone.

EIGHT

Miles felt rather stung by Clare's remarks yet he was determined to follow her advice. He made up his mind that he would go round to Kavita's home that Friday evening.

A few days before the fateful Friday, Miles was doing some sketching during the college lunch hour. The subject was a sycamore tree, its tattered arms held out against the cirrus-blown sky. Miles hoped to remain undisturbed but he soon sensed with annoyance that someone was hovering behind him.

'That's good. D'you mind if I watch?'

Miles' irritation vanished as he recognised Kamlesh's voice. 'Not at all.'

Kamlesh continued watching. Miles tried, fairly successfully, to avoid having his concentration disturbed. It suddenly struck him what a terribly nice person Kamlesh was. Most of the other boys would have made fun of him.

Miles finished, and paused for a moment for Kamlesh to look at the drawing.

'More interesting than a squashed tube, eh?' Kamlesh laughed. 'I say – I've been thinking. Could I ask you a favour?'

'Why not?'

'Well, in October us Hindus celebrate Dwali. I'll tell you all about that later. Anyway, me and my sister Kavita and some others are doing a little pageant about the story of Rama and Sita. What I want to ask you is – will you paint the scenery?'

Miles' mind was made up in a flash but he pretended to hesitate. 'Yes – yes, that'll be alright.'

'You'll have to do it for love, mind – there'll be no payment.'

'I don't want payment.'

'Right. That's agreed.'

For a moment Kamlesh touched Miles' hand rather as his sister had. 'We're having a preparation session on Monday evening. Just turn up – Unity Hall, Grimshaw Street – about seven.'

With relief, Miles realised that the Friday evening ordeal had become superfluous.

NINE

Miles knew more or less where Unity Hall was. It was in a part of the town called Luddvale on the lowest part of one of the long grey valleys that stretched like fingers towards the moors at the west. Miles had been there as a boy visiting some elderly relation fallen on bad times; the memory was vague. Yet as he left the bus that evening he realised he still remembered the close-packed, stone-built terraced houses which stepped their way up the hillside, and the cramped front gardens – not gardens, really, just strips of concrete surrounded by railings or gaunt privet hedges. In a way little had changed. Despite the smokeless zone, the houses remained uncleaned; they were still the same sooty black. Yet somehow the whole atmosphere was totally different.

It was the waft of spiced pilau coming from a steamy kitchen window and the scarlet kurtas all flapping on the washing lines that made the difference. Wesley Street, where Kavita lived, was a turning lower down Grimshaw Street. But Miles' route didn't take him that far. He merely glanced in the direction as if towards a somewhat unlikely promised land.

*

'Now we come to Dwali when we celebrate the return of Rama and Sita from the forest and the great tale of Vishnu's conflict with the forces of evil contained in the Ramayana.'

Miles laid down his brush for a moment as Manoj's soft yet carrying voice spoke the prelude across the shadows of the bare dim hall.

'At the very beginning of our story you will remember that the gods had gathered in council because they were worried about the power of Ravana, the king of the demons. He had gained this power because Brahma, impressed by Ravana's show of holiness, had promised him that he would never be slain by god, demon, spirit or serpent. Only man could kill him and Ravana wasn't worried by that because he despised man. So he wrought great evil on the earth: he destroyed the gods' pleasure gardens, carried off nymphs and celestial dancers, and disturbed the sacrifice of the blessed hermits. The gods decided that only by one of them entering into a man could Ravana be destroyed so Vishnu entered part of his spirit into the bodies of four brothers, the sons of King Dasharatha: Rama, Bharata, Shatrughna and Lakshmana. In the first scene we are at the court of King Dasharatha. He and his three queens and his four sons and their wives, are all assembled together.'

The curtain rose and there was Dasharatha at the centre of the stage – old, grey-bearded, and wearing a dhoti of gold. Yes, Dr Vyas certainly looked the sad, old man type. Around him was his entourage, a great shimmering of crowns and saris, beautiful colours juxtaposed (cerise against sea-green – that was lovely), and strange dark eyes, dark faces, glowing, handsome. Beyond all this was the scenery – the pillars, arches and windows – that Miles had started painting.

At other times he would have taken pride in this, let his eye linger on it, but right now he only had eyes for one thing – Kavita. Yet of course, she wasn't Kavita now; she was Sita, the wife of Rama, the epitome of Indian womanhood. Yes, she looked it too. It was she who was wearing that cerise sari, the one that created the exquisite contrast as she stood beside Usha, the maidservant. And her long dark hair rivered downwards across the sari's folds; her slim bronzed midriff glowed in the footlights; her dark, dark eyes, solemn in repose, radiated wild enjoyment. It was these eyes that Miles found so overwhelming – that zest, that 'child's first view of the Christmas tree' sparkle.

But for the rest of that evening, and for several other similar evenings, Miles had to be content with only the most fleeting contact with her. True, there was plenty of socialising amidst the rehearsing but Kavita was the leading lady, the centre of attention.

Miles observed her from afar. What he saw he mostly admired but there were a few things that jarred on him, such as the rather spiteful way she treated Dr Vyas, for example. The doctor was older than most of them – only in his late twenties – but he was one of the few men in the Indian community of that age who was still unmarried. The fact that he was playing Dasharatha exaggerated his age; in a way he seemed an old man and there was something cruel in the little criticisms Kavita thrust at him.

But to Miles she was always kind. She never passed him without a glance, a word, a smile. And yes, he was satisfied with these small crumbs of affection – for the present.

It was the scenery for the second act that Miles most enjoyed painting. It took place in the forest where Rama and Sita had been banished due to the machinations of Dasharatha's youngest wife, Kaikeyi. Lovingly he painted the green palm trees and the great creepers, basing his ideas on books from the library.

But time was running out. Dwali would be upon them in a fortnight's time, and the scenery was far from ready. When Kamlesh had first asked Miles, he had expected him to do a fairly simple job that merely hinted at the elaborate palace architecture and the jungle trees. Miles, however, had decided to treat it like an important commission and put everything he had into the job. It had to be worthy of the play, of Dwali. Of Kavita.

*

One Sunday morning Miles woke early. He pulled open the curtains of his small bedroom that overlooked the vicarage doorway. It was an autumn dawn; there was no sign of a sunrise, just a white diffuse light in the eastern sky. The low hills stretched out below in gradations of greyness.

Breakfast would be at eight in two hours time, matins at half ten. He thought of the unfinished scenery at Unity Hall – the forest scene. He made a decision. Without telling anyone or leaving a note, he slipped downstairs and let himself quietly out by the side door. Then he took the secluded footpath that led down the steep hill towards Holmefield.

Few people were around as Miles walked through the city. Lucky! The stage door at Unity Hall was unlocked. Soon he had assembled his paints and was absorbed in his work. For the first hour or so he continued undisturbed. He daydreamed, mainly about the story of the play, the actual Kavita and the legendary Sita somehow fused in his mind.

At ten o'clock some Indian women arrived and started setting up a sale of work in the next room. Their jabbering, high-pitched voices irritated Miles. Then a girl in jeans, plimsolls and a T-shirt walked into the room where Miles was working. Annoyed by the intrusion, he tried to carry on with the painting but the girl just stood there and watched.

Miles glanced up and to his amazement he recognised Kavita. The everyday ordinariness of her appearance stunned him. Suddenly he realised that this semi- goddess he had worshipped from afar was also a typically pretty Indian girl student –why, there were several in Miles' class almost equally attractive.

So intense was this impression that Miles struggled to collect his thoughts and think up a topic of conversation. Fortunately, Kavita was more at ease.

'I just came with my mother to bring some samosas for the sale. That door was ajar so I said to myself, "Right, I'll go and see how our great artist is getting on – whether our forest has grown another tree today or at least a shrub or a flower." My word, you are going to some trouble. Mind – I don't like this leaf up here. I shall expect it to be improved for the final event.' She pointed to a tiny splodge of green paint at the top of a tree.

Miles pretended to be interested in it and made some minute modification with the tip of his brush. 'How's that?'

'Yes, that will do for the time being. But everything must be perfect for the big night. Perfect, do you hear?'

As she spoke, Kavita was never still. She stood on her toes, she waved her arms, she pointed at every object she referred to.

'You are eternally dancing.'

'Yes, I am. D'you know, every year before I have been one of the dancing troupe in this play. It seems strange to be acting – though of course it's a great honour to play Sita. Last year I was one of the troupe of monkeys. I spent all the play swinging in the trees like this...'

Kavita lifted her graceful arms and went on tiptoe like a monkey going along a branch and supporting itself on the branch above.

'The year before, I was Jatayu the vulture. That was great fun. I had to attack Ravana when he abducted Sita. My eldest brother Amrish was playing Ravana. D'you know, I fought so furiously I actually gave him a real scratch right down his arm which drew blood. Oh yes' – she clapped her hands – 'I must show you my first part. That was when I was a tiny little girl back in India, near Bombay. I was a jackal. See...'

Kavita fell down on her hands and knees and rushed towards Miles, barking. At that moment Miles heard the sound of footsteps approaching the door. Kavita leapt up abruptly. 'Heavens – my mother. She'll think me mad.'

A quite elderly wizened lady entered the room wearing a pale green kurta and a dupatta to match. Kavita hastily brushed the dust off her knees.

'Oh, Mother, I was just showing Miles here my jackal dance. It's lucky you came in – I might have got so carried away I would have bitten a hole in the scenery. Oh yes...' Kavita suddenly remembered her manners. 'I must introduce you. My mother – Miles. Miles is a very close friend of Kamlesh, Mother, and he's painting the scenery for our play.'

Miles wasn't sure that this was all strictly true but he took the woman's hand and looked into her face. Vaguely he wondered how such an elderly lady could possibly be Kavita's mother. Had she ever once been as young and beautiful as her daughter? Would Kavita... But no, never mind.

'So you are a close friend of Kamlesh?'

'Yes,' interjected Kavita, 'I've – we've tried to persuade Miles to visit us but he doesn't come. I think he's shy.' She put her hand teasingly on Miles' arm and smiled her dimple-puckered smile.

'Oh, you mustn't be shy,' said the mother. 'If you are a friend of Kamlesh, you are always welcome at our house. Where do you live?'

'Tostenland.'

'Tostenland,' Kavita repeated. 'Dr Vyas's girlfriend – woman friend or whatever – lives there. How funny! Do you know her? They call her Sheila, Sheila Field.'

'A bit, but I know her sister Clare much better.'

'Oh. And is Clare another of these blonde-haired blue-eyed English girls?'

'Yes – she's much more attractive than her sister.'

'Well, God help her if Dr Vyas ever claps eyes on her. He's just mad on English girls. The blonder the hair, the bluer the eyes, the better he likes them. And not just girls, anything English – English cars, English cooking, English films – it's all got to be English. I tease him mercilessly about it.'

She darted a glance at Miles that he couldn't quite interpret. There was an embarrassed silence for a few moments. 'Anyway,' said Kavita breaking it, 'we must get back and start cooking the pilau. We'd invite you for lunch but we already have visitors. Come round one evening – say Thursday, about six. Alright, Mother?'

The wizened lady nodded.

'See you.' Kavita waved in the doorway and smiled that weasel-like smile of hers.

Miles went back to his painting but he couldn't concentrate any longer – the brush actually trembled in his hand. That first impression of ordinariness had quickly worn off. No, Kavita wasn't ordinary; she was anything but ordinary. Even in jeans and a T-shirt she was so Indian and so enchanting – more than enchanting. So utterly and terribly alive.

Soon Miles gave up pretending to paint and went off back home.

TEN

Miles was happy as he walked home. He could have taken the bus but he preferred to walk along the small lanes and footpaths that led back up the hill to Tostenland. Mid-September, with just a hint of the leaves turning colour and with the wet heads of the uncut barley still waiting for a late harvest. But Miles saw little of this. He was picturing Kavita rushing at him in imitation of a jackal and all the other minute details of their meeting.

Lunch started silently that day. The main course of beef and Yorkshire pudding was laid on the plates like a quiet ritual.

'You weren't at matins this morning,' said his stepfather.

'No.'

'Why not?'

'I went to Unity Hall to paint the scenery for the play celebrating Dwali.'

'Dwali?'

'It's the time when the Hindus celebrate the return of Rama and Sita from the forest.'

'Oh, of course – of course. I remember from my missionary days.'

For a moment Miles hoped that the vicar would just launch into some reminiscences of his time in India. But no.

'Hmm. I don't mind you taking an interest in comparative religion – but your first allegiance must be to the Lord Jesus Christ.'

Miles didn't reply but continued attacking his Yorkshire pudding in silence.

*

Miles did little for the next few hours except daydream. The afternoon turned cloudy and a sudden shower towards evening cast a great double rainbow, vivid and fresh against the eastern sky. The bell for evensong rang out. He resented it.

The clearing clouds gave every promise of a fine evening. 'Damn it,' Miles thought. 'I'll miss evensong as well.'

Despite all the walking of the morning he decided to go out yet again but he felt the need for some justification, so he thrust a drawing pad under his arm.

He hadn't gone far when he met Clare walking towards him wearing riding breeches and carrying a saddle. She paused at the gate of the paddock where Tara and Gerda were grazing. Gerda was her sister Sheila's pony, a fine piebald.

'Going riding?' Miles asked, realising it was an obvious question.

'Yes. Why aren't you at evensong?'

'I wasn't in the mood. I decided to take a walk instead.'

'Why don't you come riding with me then?'

'Riding? But I don't know that I could – I've only ridden a few times. And I haven't the gear.'

'Oh, it will soon come back to you. You can use Gerda – she's terribly docile and Sheila won't mind. As for the gear, that doesn't really matter. You stay here and I'll slip back to the stable for Gerda's saddle.'

Clare soon returned and they rode off together. Miles felt unsure of himself and yet exhilarated. It was the strange movement of Gerda's haunches on the uneven ground; the closeness of Clare as they brushed together in the narrow bridleway; the beauty of the evening as the clouds cleared and the first stars flowered in the darkening east. They rode steeply down into the valley, the tall bracken brushing against their knees, then up the far side through a woodland ride between sitka spruces. They emerged onto a wide span of heather-clad moorland. Ahead of them in the west, long scarecrow tatters of clouds were flushed by a crimson sun.

They stopped.

'Isn't this splendid?' Clare said. 'D'you know, if I wasn't a Christian I'd be a pantheist and believe that God was in all nature – like Wordsworth.'

'Perhaps I already do,' answered Miles. 'That sunset does more for me spiritually than all the matins and evensongs. Did I tell you? I've missed both today.'

'I noticed you weren't at matins. I went with Mother. It's funny – I feel so apart from Mother at the moment and yet we've got all this Christian belief in common. It ought to be a wonderful bond. But it isn't – not now, at any rate.'

'I thought you said once that you were a rebel.'

'Well, I am! Why do you query it?'

'Because in the most important things of life you just go along with what your parents have taught you. You may be a rebel in the trivialities – what you wear, those long colourful dresses and bright ponchos – but in the essentials you're a traditionalist. I mean, it's what one believes that really matters.'

'Yes, maybe I am. Christianity certainly means a lot to me – in fact, it's the centre of my life. But somehow I want to follow Christ in my own way, in a spirit of liberty, not through restrictions and ritual.'

'Why do you go to church then?'

'Hmm – it's funny, isn't it? But really I love it. That experience you get some mornings when the sunlight is streaming through the "Lord Is My Shepherd" window, and somewhere beyond the song of the birds blends in with the hymns.'

'I know what you mean but I somehow feel a growing impatience with religion – or at any rate with the sort of sentimental Christianity that my mother lives in. The creative spirit – that's my religion. Painting: it's a sort of act of worship.'

'But somehow to me Jesus Christ is a real person, a friend I can talk to and get guidance from when my thoughts are divided. I feel when I pray that there is someone there at the other end, someone really there – talking back to me.'

There was a pause. Clare was looking at the sunset now; Miles had his back to it and was only looking at Clare. He hardly heard her theological observations. He glanced at her form and thought how fine she was: her strong but slim thighs pressed into Tara's flanks; her prominent breasts, sloping shoulders, long neck, blue eyes. But above all it was her glossy fair hair, the way it tumbled from below her black riding cap and fell downwards almost to her hips.

Was she more beautiful than Kavita? He couldn't say. Kavita's was the beauty of the east – dark, exotic, fascinating. Clare's beauty was utterly English, as English as a Constable painting or the scene beyond her, where a single silver birch, the last tree before the windswept moorland, stretched its white and sepia trunk against the gathering greys of the Fielden Valley.

Suddenly, from somewhere out in the misting evening, a bell started chiming. It could have been any one of a number of churches that thrust their grey spires at the evening sky. It was puzzling to hear it now, far too late to be a summons for evensong. Miles heard it as a rebuke. For some reason, which he couldn't have explained, he abruptly said, 'Shall we go now?'

'No,' Clare replied quite sharply, ameliorating the impression immediately with a smile. 'No – I'm very happy here with you and the ponies, watching that sunset. I want to wait until the last edge of the sun has disappeared over Scapegoat Hill. I love that time when you see the red disc just perched above the dark hill and then it slips down so quickly.'

'Yes,' Miles said weakly, wondering why he had ever suggested otherwise.

'Have you seen Kavita recently?' Clare shot the question, arrow-like.

'Yes – yes,' Miles answered brightening.

'And things are hopeful?'

'I think so. It was this morning. She was delightful – showed me some of her dances. Oh, and she's asked me round to her house on Thursday.'

'I'm so glad.'

'You take a lot of interest in my well-being.'

'I am your friend. Doesn't that explain it?'

'I suppose it does.'

'I only wish my own life were as hopeful.'

'What's the matter?'

'I've quarrelled with Nat.'

'I'm sorry – is it serious?'

'I don't know. I hope not, because I've always felt that Nat was the right person for me.'

Miles felt more interest in this information than he cared to admit. He was embarrassed by his own interest. Whilst the conversation paused tensely, the sunset reached the point that Clare had described and they both watched the scarlet disc vanish. When it was gone, a darkness seemed to descend not just over the landscape but over their spirits as well.

'Let's go back,' Clare said.

ELEVEN

It was the question of how Kavita would be dressed that engaged Miles' thoughts as he walked down Grimshaw Street through the thin autumn rain in the direction of Wesley Street. He had never even walked past her house; all he knew was the whereabouts of Wesley Street and the house number – sixteen. But he had already pictured the green-painted door swinging open and Kavita standing there in the passage in her cerise sari, like Sita emerging from the darkness of the forest. Or perhaps she would just rush breathlessly to the door in her jeans, T-shirt and plimsolls, the goddess of the ordinary. He though it would be very significant how she was dressed yet he wasn't sure which he would prefer.

He turned the corner of Wesley Street and there was Vora General Stores, red lettering on a green ground, about halfway down. He glanced at the window. Cereal packets, toilet rolls, washing-up liquid; vaguely he tried to fit all this into Kavita's world. Sixteen was next door but the door wasn't green, it was just a slab of frosted glass.

He rang the bell. After a few moments he could see Kavita coming forward. Her form looking like a cubist painting as the glass deflected the image.

The door swung open and there she was, exactly as he had pictured: same sari, same everything. But no. There was something wrong; the face was fractionally too old, too coarse to be Kavita.

The face smiled at his puzzlement. 'You took me for Kavita, didn't you? Just for an instant? I'm Indu, her eldest sister. We're often confused. But Kavita's prettier. Remember that and you won't go wrong.'

Miles stepped into the house, momentarily at a loss for words.

'Oh yes – go into the living room,' Indu continued. 'Kavita won't be long.'

As he stepped forward, Miles reflected that although he had been invited as a friend of the family, more particularly of Kamlesh, the sister took it for granted that he had come to see Kavita.

He entered the living room. It was surprisingly large, extending right to the back of the house. The walls and ceiling were of discoloured white. On the floor was a rich red carpet that was worn threadbare beneath the chairs and tables. The sofa and easy chairs were of similarly worn upholstery. In one corner a black-and-white television was on – a cartoon film – watched by three rather scruffy little children. There was a bookcase and, above it on shelves, metal statuettes of Siva and Vishnu, Rama and Sita. A candle was burning in front of Rama. On the walls were many pictures, some framed and hung, others merely stuck on with Blu Tack. Amongst the former was a rather poor portrait of a young man; a garland was hung around it. Amongst the latter were posters of David Bowie and Michael Jackson.

Indu noticed Miles looking at these. 'Oh, that's another sister, Aditi – she's number four. Aditi's into all this pop stuff. Kavita's quite different. She's the baby of the family – and the most old-fashioned. Funny, isn't it? And then she's so pretty that everyone spoils her – they always have. Did she tell you there are eight of us? Five girls and three boys. My second brother, Rajin' – she nodded at the portrait with the garland – 'he died young. We still miss him. Three of the girls are married. There's only Aditi and Kavita left but there's a young man they want Aditi to marry in Birmingham. She'll meet him for the first time next weekend. Oh, and these three are all mine I'm afraid,' she added, nodding at the trio on the carpet.

Miles sat down on the sofa and tried to absorb this potted family history. Indu advanced towards the television and abruptly switched it off.

'I was watching that! Now I won't know what's happened,' screamed a little girl, jumping up.

'You mustn't be selfish, Lata. This gentleman doesn't want to watch Yogi Bear.'

'Yes – it's all because of him,' Lata shouted, darting a pair of malevolent black eyes towards Miles.

'Oh, please don't switch it off because of me,' said Miles, embarrassed.

Lata stamped her tiny foot on the threadbare carpet and her mother hit her on the forearm. The blow was only gentle but it brought on a monsoon of tears. In the midst of the chaos, Kavita entered.

As so often in life, the reality proves to be neither of the extremes one had envisaged. Kavita wore neither the rich sari nor the tatty jeans. Instead she had on a salwar of plain blue and over it a kurta of the same colour but with a pattern in darker blue.

Ignoring the childish dispute, Kavita advanced towards Miles and said something about being pleased to see him, which he only half heard through Lata's sobbing. He was almost glad of Lata's outburst because it took the embarrassment and formality out of the situation. Kavita sat on the sofa and took her niece on her lap. She stroked the child's hair and asked what was the matter. Lata poured out her grievance at some length.

'But there's a repeat on Friday evening,' Kavita said.

'Yes, but I'm not allowed to stay up so late.'

'You will be. If you're a good girl now, I'll especially plead for you. You know I can always get my own way when I try.' Kavita smiled at Miles.

Lata's crying stopped as abruptly as it had started. The child suddenly seemed to sense that she was in the way and, without another word, slid from Kavita's lap and followed her two brothers and her mother out of the room.

For a moment Miles felt a strange panic at finding himself alone with Kavita. He tried to persuade himself that this was the moment he had been waiting for. But the silence was brief.

'So, you shy boy, we have persuaded you to come round at last,' Kavita said.

'Yes. It seems ages since you asked me – as a friend of the family.'

At the words 'friend of the family' Kavita looked straight in his face and gave him one of her more ambivalent smiles. For a moment it was a mocking smile, as if she saw straight through his bluff and wanted to make fun of him. Then her look changed to something gentle and tender; she understood his secret, welcomed it, wanted to reassure him. In an instant Miles realised that Kavita wasn't someone to be worshipped from afar. He could be very close to her, not see her as something from a different world, and they could look out on all the worlds together.

Then Kavita made her characteristic gesture: she touched the back of his hand. Her eyes shifted hastily from his to the room, to the toys scattered all over the floor. 'Oh what a terrible mess! All those toys – those horrid children! Oh no – I love them really. Never mind, we'll have a big clean-up for Dwali.'

'How will you celebrate Dwali? I mean, I know what it signifies because of the play but what do you do at home?'

'Well, let me think.' Kavita pressed her hands together and cast her eyes upwards as if seeking divine guidance. 'It's difficult to answer. Everything is so different in England.' She threw her hands apart. 'Ten years ago, back in India, when I was a little girl of seven – oh, then we did so many things. We sent cards, exchanged gifts, us children let off fireworks, and then we welcomed the Goddess Laxmi to our homes with marigold garlands over the door and a very special design on the doorstep. Look, I will show you.' She picked up a bit of child's chalk and, sitting on the floor, she drew a symbol on the tattered carpet.

'But that's a swastika.'

'No, no, not a swastika. A swastika has the arms pointing the other way. No, this is an Indian religious symbol. And then alongside we draw these – these are the footsteps of the goddess.' She shrugged. 'But in England we don't do these things. Perhaps just a few close friends come round for a meal, nothing more. But then, of course, there is the play. The play – that's great. I'm looking forward to it so much, playing Sita. And you've taken so much trouble over the scenery. Kamlesh expected you to do a few simple designs but you've made it into a work of art.'

'I enjoyed it.'

'But isn't it funny, an English clergyman's son doing the scenery for a Hindu play? Haven't you been criticised?'

'Yes, I have been actually.'

'Oh dear, I hope you won't get into trouble.'

'Nothing serious. Nothing that matters.' At the back of his mind he was saying, 'Nothing I wouldn't do for you,' but he repressed it.

'And the play is close now – only a week. You will come, won't you?'

'Yes, of course.'

'Will you bring a friend?'

'I don't know. I can't think who I could bring.'

'Anyway, you know all of us. You can come round and see me when the play is over. Don't forget.'

There was a footstep in the hall. Kamlesh entered shyly, quietly. Miles had spent a good half hour alone with Kavita and he appreciated Kamlesh's tact. Now Kamlesh came forward and held out his hand. It was strange – one didn't shake hands with one's school friends. But Miles realised this was significant. It was the old Indian courtesy – and something more.

Kamlesh pulled up a chair and talked with them for some while. He talked of India. He and Kavita reminisced about all the places they had been to but somehow to Miles it seemed to have another meaning beyond the words, something unexpressed.

Soon afterwards, the meal was served. Miles was placed between Kavita and Kamlesh. All the foods were explained to him and he tried hard to remember their names but towards the end of the meal these names had begun to blur in a confused mass. His confusion was further increased by all the people who dropped in and had to be introduced. Miles realised that the Voras' house was one of those homes where people just dropped in without any need for a motive or an invitation. They appeared in the living room, socialised for as long as they wished and then went,

Amongst these droppers-in was Dr Vyas, 'Dr Fuss' as Kavita called him behind his back. Miles noticed the deference with which her parents treated him. There was something almost servile in the way Mr Vora placed his hand on the young man's shoulder, expressed admiration for his new suit and ushered him to the best chair. The doctor glanced at Miles, a quizzical, deprecating look, as if he were wondering what Miles' presence at the family table signified. And after Dr Vyas was gone they sang his praises, mentioning all the important committees he was involved in. Only Kavita failed to join in this adulation; even in the presence of her parents she was only acidly polite to the dapper man.

But all this vast confusion of foods and names and people didn't dispirit Miles. He had Kavita by his side and her physical closeness made him feel safe, secure. When she briefly left the room, he felt utterly helpless.

Finally it was time to go. Kamlesh and Kavita came with him to the door. Kamlesh held back and Miles was alone on the doorstep with Kavita. He took her hand.

For a moment he wondered if he should kiss her. Did you kiss an Indian girl? He wasn't sure.

'See you at Diwali,' Kavita said.

'I hope it will be a happy Dwali.'

'It will be.'

She waved and Miles walked back down the dark cobbles of Wesley Street, confused, happy.

TWELVE

In a way, the Dwali play itself was an anti-climax for Miles. Everything had been accomplished beforehand as far as he was concerned. The scenery had been painted; he had done a good job of it and everyone had praised it. But what was far more important to Miles was that this little commission had formed a bridgehead to Kavita. She was no longer the stranger she had been before Kamlesh had asked for that favour. No; now Miles could visit her at her home whenever he wished. That right was accepted, unchallenged.

Yet he was puzzled by the very easiness of everything. How did the bond between them appear to the outside world? How did it appear to themselves? He wasn't sure.

But the evening of the play's performance was a success, there was no doubt about that. The acting, dancing, costumes, scenery – all were beautiful. How could it have been otherwise when so much enthusiasm had gone into it? There was a big audience and every seat was taken, not just by Indians – lots of English people were there. And yes, there was one thing that was very special about the evening for Miles: he was able to introduce Clare to Kavita. Clare was there with Sheila.

As soon as the play was over, Sheila went off to talk to Dr Vyas. Miles went across to Clare and led her towards the back of the stage. When they got there, they found Kavita surrounded by a great hoard of sisters, brothers, nieces, cousins, aunts and friends. Miles almost despaired of pushing Clare and himself through the mêlée but by waiting to one side until the enthusiasm of Kavita's fans had subsided, they eventually reached the great lady herself.

Miles introduced them. The two girls touched hands for a moment, exchanged a few polite conventional sentences, but what they said didn't matter. Miles stood to one side, noticing the beautiful contrast as Clare's turquoise dress rested against the cerise of Kavita's sari. They had met. This was terribly significant. But why? He couldn't say.

THIRTEEN

The chestnuts were the first to turn that year. Clare, from her bedroom window, watched every morning as the one by the farmyard's edge modulated from its summer green until its edges were sunrise-scarlet against the misted woodland. Sheila's window faced the other way, westward towards the steep hillside; whether for this reason, or because she had a less zestful view of living, she usually rose later than her younger sister.

On this particular morning, when the chestnut seemed to have reached its maximum possible brilliance, Clare was already on her bacon and mushrooms when Sheila entered the kitchen. Despite being the elder sister, Sheila was smaller, her hair and skin somewhat darker.

'Have you seen how red the chestnut is – not the whole tree, just that one branch?' Clare asked.

'Never mind the beauties of nature. I'm starving. Where's the tea? It's not in the right-hand cupboard.'

'No, it's in the left-hand one.'

'Well, why can't you put it away in the correct place? You are untidy.'

'Alright, I'm untidy and you're tidy. I like wearing bright colours and you like wearing dull ones. Does it matter?'

'It does when you're trying to find something.'

'Got out of bed the wrong side this morning?'

'Slightly – only slightly. Nothing that a morning's walk won't put right.'

'Yes, it looks hopeful. Once the mist is cleared it should be lovely.'

Sheila started her breakfast whilst Clare looked wistfully at the autumn colours. Their mother's footsteps came fussily down and then, with a far slower tread, their father's.

The mother entered the kitchen and immediately began making comments to herself. Sheila got her temperament from her mother, this eternal fussing over trivia. Clare was more like her father: calm. But with Clare it was the calmness of serenity; with her father the calmness of a strange despair.

He stood now, silently, at the kitchen window. Like his younger daughter, he noticed the chestnut and looked at it intently. But he seemed to see something other than the beauty that Clare noticed – a sadness, a dying away. He was an old man to have such a young daughter, just turned sixty and thinking of early retirement from his job as an architect. Years ago, when he was only a lad of twenty, he had received a bad wound in the thigh during the last weeks of the Second World War. It gave him a permanent limp. Slowly the wound in his thigh seemed to have spread over his whole spirit. Clare had been begotten in the last flowering of his will to live before the terrible desolation became complete.

He turned from the window and sat down at the table just as Sheila finished her breakfast. She glanced across at her younger sister and Clare could see that the brief ill humour had already passed.

'Let's go for a walk.'

'Off already are you?' scolded the mother.

'It's alright. You can leave the washing up,' Sheila answered the implied criticism.

Their mother merely shrugged; their father looked blankly before him.

Had Sheila's pony not been lame, they would have gone riding. As it was, they walked along the high path that followed the saddle towards Height's Farm and Farnley Plump. The rooks were cawing in the yellowing sycamores around the vicarage. There was no sign of Miles, but his stepfather could be seen sitting in his study.

'I wonder what that shy boy is doing this morning,' Clare said.

'Why do you call him "that shy boy"?'

'Oh that's Kavita's expression, so I gather. It's her way of teasing him.'

'Do you think he is a shy boy?'

'In a way. But like most shy people, he's got a terribly extrovert side to his nature that's struggling to get out.'

'Perhaps Kavita will open the doors for it.'

'Maybe. He's absolutely mad on her.'

'I hope he doesn't get hurt. Those shy intense people are so vulnerable.'

'Aren't we all vulnerable?' Clare gave a darting glance with her blue eyes as she asked the question.

'I don't know.' Sheila looked down. 'I try to protect myself. I must say, you've got over Nat pretty quickly.'

'Yes, I know. It was one of those things that seemed terribly important at the time but now it's over it just doesn't matter. I thought I was going to be very hurt but somehow the hurt vanished and now I feel quite healthy again.'

'You've got more resilience than I have. I like to keep life under control in case the storm gets too violent and I capsize.'

'You seem pretty keen on Dr Vyas.'

A look rather like pain came into Sheila's eyes. 'Well, yes, I feel something – flattered, perhaps. He's a very clever man, there's no doubt, kind too – the way he treats his mother. But – well, where will it all end? I'm trying to control it, keep it at arm's length.'

'I don't think you can keep life under control. It's a wayward stallion that's never been broken in. No good tugging on the reins – let it charge off where it will. Maybe it will take you to some beautiful hillside. Maybe it will throw you in the ditch. No good worrying beforehand – just let it go.'

'I wish Gerda wasn't lame and we could be riding now,' Sheila said, reminded of the more mundane aspects of horse riding.

'I don't know. You notice different things when you're walking – the dew on the grass and those beautiful cobwebs in the hedge.'

'Yes, they are lovely. But I'm tired. Can't we rest somewhere?'

'Maybe – but everything's so damp.'

They had come to a spot where a narrow strip of woodland ran along the hilly plateau and below stretched slopes of rough grass with a few gorse bushes and brambles. The view of the valley beyond was extensive and an artist had placed his easel on a relatively level patch and was busy painting.

'Oh that's Randal, Randal Bramley,' exclaimed Clare. 'He's quite a famous artist, you know.'

'I'll take your word. It's you that knows all these artists.'

'Shall we go and talk to him?'

'If you really want to.'

'Of course, he may not want to be disturbed.'

But as she spoke, Randal turned his head. The smile breaking out above the auburn beard seemed welcoming enough. 'Hello,' he said.

'Hello. Will we put you off if we stand and watch you for a bit?'

'Not at all. I find people who disturb me when I've just started are a pest. But once I'm firmly launched, nothing matters. I'm absorbed and that's that.'

Randal wasn't painting a general view of the valley as they had expected but was concentrating on a small gnarled oak tree that grew close by. When they looked at the canvas, however, they realised that although the actual tree was the starting point, Randal was interpreting it imaginatively, exaggerating the twisted shape, enlarging the brown, withered leaves that still clung to it. Was it perhaps a picture of a struggle, a rear-guard action, as autumn fought off the inevitable arrival of winter?

Clare and Sheila stood for quite some while, watching. Randal seemed to have forgotten all about them so absorbed was he in his work. Just once he appeared to reach a point where the next move was uncertain. He looked up, cast a long glance at Clare, and then resumed furiously as if he had read the answer to his private dilemma somewhere in the blueness of her eyes.

Finally the picture was finished. Randal laid it on one side to dry for a bit and then began cleaning up his brushes with turps and an old rag.

'Do you usually paint abstract or representational subjects?' Sheila asked, trying to enter into the spirit of the thing.

'A sort of in between really. Actuality's always the starting point.'

Randal looked back at his little gnarled oak as if he had again forgotten the sisters. Then he fumbled in an inside pocket and took out a card. 'Anyway, if you want to see more of my work here's an invite to the opening of my next exhibition.'

He held out the card towards the sisters and then, with the slightest movement, stretched his hand closer to Clare. She took the card, smiled. Sheila, feeling cut out by this tiny gesture, looked down at the mill-spiked greyness of the valley. The promise of the brilliant morning had faded and slow dark clouds were sneaking in from above the Pennines. Then Clare noticed something falling and landing at her feet.

'The first snowflake,' she said, turning to Randal.

FOURTEEN

Winter set in early that year. The first snowflake, the one that fell at Clare's feet, was a prelude to a series of clean frosted nights, followed by abrupt intense snow flurries. They soon melted in the valleys but left the Pennines clear and white, looking so much higher – high, clean, white, very white.

It was on one such cold night that Miles made his way to Kamlesh's eighteenth-birthday celebration that was to be held in a small underground night club in the centre of town. The venue surprised him – in fact the whole event surprised him. At least half the people there were Indian but there was nothing of Indian culture about the party, not a thing. The music was all disco, modern pop pulsing echoes from the polished floor and the lilac-coloured walls. No signs of a sari, not even a kurta or dupatta; all wore the sacred costume of late-twentieth-century youth – jeans and T-shirts. And there were so many people. How could Mr and Mrs Vora afford it, Miles wondered. The shop must be doing well.

At first the party disappointed Miles. One met people more by accident in the crush than by any intent. Conversation was impossible – the music slaughtered every word. He thought he glimpsed Kavita from afar but she was immediately lost again. Miles danced indifferently for a while with a girl named Tessa but eventually the random gyrations of the dance floor, twirling like a galaxy in space, brought him close to a familiar T shirt – the one Kavita had worn when she rushed at him barking in her jackal imitation. It had 'Choose Life' written across it; Miles hadn't noticed that before.

As soon as was politely possible, he left Tessa and pushed through to where Kavita was standing with Kamlesh. He tried to say something but Madonna was screaming out 'Get into the groove'. Impossible. Instead he just squeezed her hand and led her to the dance floor, and there they danced on and on until the very end of the party.

This was the other Kavita he was with now. Not the semi-goddess, not Sita the eternal woman; nothing of that. This was Kavita Vora, the second-year student at Springwood College who was studying History, Geography and English at A level. The English Kavita – in fact not just English but Yorkshire in some ways: little turns of speech she used, the way she only hinted at her 'thes' Yorkshire style. Miles found it so funny coming from her dark Indian lips.

Not that there was any scope for talking right now – the music ruined that. They just danced away, modern – no body touching, while the brilliant lights flashed and darkened. And then abruptly the heavy rock beat ceased and the disc jockey put on a slow smoochy waltz. The lights dimmed. What should he do? Was it all right to treat an Indian girl like that? He glanced round, hesitated. But Kavita had already stretched out her arms and in a moment she was close against him as they slowly made their way around the dance hall.

It was beautiful. Even the slight smell of her sweat blending in with the cheap perfume was beautiful – yes, and the pressure of her small breasts. He ran his hand down her back. As his fingers touched on her vertebrae, he thought for a moment of that nameless girl at the art class: the way the evening sunlight had cast highlights and shadows on her body. He looked in Kavita's dark, dark eyes and she smiled like a half-contented tigress.

Then, quite abruptly, the smooching stopped. The throb of rock again broke its waves on their ear drums. The lights flashed on and off, violently, giddily.

*

It was late when the party ended. They came out and stood for a few moments in the freezing chill. The flood-lit clock on the parish church looked down at them like a great moon that had taken control of the moonless night. It struck one o'clock.

There were about ten of them together – Kamlesh and his closest friends and family. They began walking through the empty streets towards the Voras' home. Miles walked beside Kavita. He would have liked to hold her hand or put his arm around her but no – something told him not to, not just then, anyway. He and Kavita said little; an odd shyness had come between them as soon as they got out into the cold night. So they walked on, the only sound that of their shoes on the pavement, the only lights those of the street lamps and a glimmering above of the brightest stars.

Suddenly Kamlesh and Aditi stopped and began looking at the sky.

'What are you waiting for?' shouted Indu. 'The next reincarnation of Vishnu?'

'No, we're looking for the comet. It's supposed to be visible about now.'

Brother and sister looked aimlessly at the sky.

'It's going to be close to Pegasus,' said Miles. He had read a bit about astronomy. 'But it's no use looking for it from here – the street lights are far too bright. The only hope would be up towards the hills.'

'Yes,' Kamlesh said enthusiastically. 'Let's go up onto Horsfall Moor and see it. I'm in no mood to go to bed – too excited. I want to see the comet on my birthday.'

'But it isn't your birthday anymore. That was yesterday.'

'Oh, never mind – it's the same night. I want to see it all bright and rushing along with a great tail sweeping across the sky, celebrating my eighteenth birthday.'

'It won't be like that,' put in Miles. 'We'll be lucky to see it at all without binoculars.'

'My dad's got some binoculars,' said Tim, whose home lay close to where they were passing. 'I'll slip in and borrow them.'

The group waited and soon Tim reappeared with the binoculars. They continued walking, past the Voras' house and on up to Horsfall Moor, which wasn't a true moor but an area of high ground above the valley. Here, close to the edge of the golf course, the street lights finished.

Most of the party stopped at this point and a mild squabble broke out as to who should use the binoculars. But without a word being said, Kavita carried on walking. Miles, too, felt his step obey some unspoken command and walked on beside her. They didn't speak, not a word. The street lights behind them dimmed and vanished. Down below, the neon lights of the Moorchester Road snaked up the valley floor but, as they moved away from the edge, these too disappeared until there was only the great canopy of clear cold stars to break the darkness,

Miles was excited. What should he do? He stretched out his hand. He could hardly see Kavita and the hand touched her shoulder. No resistance, none at all. A strand of her hair tickled teasingly against his face and then, before he could do any more, Kavita flung her arms round his waist, held him close and kissed him.

'I want you to know something, Miles,' she said.

'What's that?'

'That I love you.'

'But you always tease me. You always call me "your shy boy".'

'That's my way.'

'And what about all these problems – you being an Indian girl, religion – all that sort of thing.'

'Haven't I just told you that I love you?' She spoke almost angrily. 'Didn't you hear it? I know myself a little bit. I know the things that are superficial to me, Miles, and the ones that go right down into me like roots. Whatever problems we might have, remember I love you. Do you hear?' She held him close with a tigerish ferocity.

'And I love you.'

'I thought you did. I had a sort of feeling!' He couldn't see her but he knew she was smiling that weasel-like smile – the one where a dimple puckered above her cheek, as well as below. She gave a tiny laugh and they relapsed into the silence of a long, long embrace.

*

Eventually Miles surfaced as if from an underworld of darkened joy. Kavita was just a form, felt but not seen, except for the whites of her eyes. He looked beyond and could just make out a flag on the golf course, limp in windless air. He looked up. 'Guess what I can see?'

Kavita released her embrace and turned to look in the same direction.

'The comet!' she shouted, clapping her hands with childish joy. And there it was, not so disappointing after all: a clearly defined comet and a long tail sweeping right across the constellation of Pegasus.

'It's beautiful,' Kavita said. 'Oh, I'm so glad we've seen it. I feel so happy tonight and seeing that in the sky sort of crowns it all. But somewhere I've heard it said that comets are forewarnings of disaster. Oh yes – I know where I heard it. History. Harold saw a comet before he got an arrow in his eye at Hastings.'

'Do you think this one is a bringer of disaster?'

'I hope not – oh, I do so much hope not.' And then, despite her avowal of happiness, Kavita felt a chill come over her and she put her arms back round Miles to feel warm again in the closeness of his body.

They stayed like that for some time then Kavita suddenly roused herself. 'We'd better go,' she said and added, 'but how are you going to get home? I wonder how late it is? Here, let me see my watch. Oh – it's too dark to make out.'

They walked to the first street lamp. Kavita stopped and looked at her watch.

'Heavens! Four o'clock in the morning.' A look of fear came into her eyes for a moment. 'D'you know, I could be in serious trouble if I were seen alone with you at this time – or at any time. My parents are liberal to a point – but only to a point. Beyond that they can be quite severe.'

'I could leave you now,' Miles said. But the thought of Kavita walking back through the streets alone troubled him. 'No, I'll see you to your door.'

'But what will you do?'

'I'll walk home.'

'Walk?'

'Yes, I like walking. And tomorrow's Saturday. I can sleep it off.'

They walked back silently through the empty streets.

'Will you get in?' Miles asked.

'Yes. We always keep a spare key under a flowerpot in the shed. Goodnight.'

They didn't kiss; a hurried squeeze of the hand and she was off.

Miles walked back through the darkness. By the time he reached the hill above Tostenland the late winter dawn was already breaking. It was mostly pink, with purple clouds above the soft chilled light catching on the snow-skiffs above the dark stone walls. Birds twittered coldly, very coldly and quietly, somewhere in the leafless woods.

FIFTEEN

Clare looked musingly at the small snowflakes slowly building little dips and arches against the window of Randal's studio. She had to stay still for the portrait but she let her eyes wander around; she watched Randal's daughter, Yvette, only five years younger than herself, nipping in hastily and grabbing an apple from the fruit bowl; she looked at the little robin that had perched cheekily on the garden fence; she rested her eyes on the slow curves of the quickly whitening hills. It would soon be Christmas.

Clare was wearing her blue dress – Randal had insisted on that – the ideal contrast to her long fair hair. Normally he only painted commissioned portraits but this was different. He had met Clare and Sheila again at the exhibition opening. From a few joking remarks had come this decision to paint her portrait. No one paid anyone; it was just done for its own sake.

Clare sensed that Randal had done as much as he intended for that day but nonetheless she remained still for a few moments. Then she moved her head slightly, tossed back her hair and looked questioningly.

'Oh yes, you can move now,' Randal said. 'There's me treating you as if you were a bowl of fruit.'

'Thanks. It's quite a relief to move. I was feeling almost that I *was* a bowl of fruit.' Clare stood up and straightened her dress with a quick downward movement of her palms. Then she went and stood at the window. 'My word, all that snow already this year and it's still falling. Winter's come early.'

'Yes, and you walked over didn't you. Perhaps I could give you a lift back. There's the Land Rover – it's ideal for this weather.'

'Oh no, I love the snow. I get a tremendous sense of well-being when the snow's on the ground. Every second of life seems precious and beautiful. Do you ever feel like that?'

The slightly gloomy look that often wintered on Randal's features seemed to melt. He smiled at the question's directness. 'Yes, sometimes. Not often. But then I'm a lot older. There's been more time for things to go wrong in life.'

'I can't understand anyone being unhappy when the world seems so beautiful. Look at that magpie flying up against the sky and those icicles dangling from the stone wall. Do you ever paint snow scenes?'

'Mostly I use scraperboard for snow – it seems more suitable. But yes, I have done a few oils. I can show you.'

They withdrew from the window and approached a door at the end of the studio that Clare hadn't been through before. Randal seemed to hesitate. 'The kitchen will be a right mess.'

He pushed open the door. Yvette was sitting by the electric fire supposedly doing her homework, textbooks and exercise books scattered everywhere. But she was really looking at a record sleeve, or rather listening to a record and studying the sleeve at the same time. Clare recognised Joan Baez singing 'Mary Hamilton', the melancholy song filling the small room. Yvette looked up at

Clare and tugged guiltily at her auburn hair then let her violet eyes and freckled cheeks slip into a sly smile.

Randal glanced beyond his daughter at the pile of unwashed dishes, turned and looked apologetically at Clare. But she understood. She knew Randal had been a widower for five years; one couldn't do everything.

Beyond the kitchen they came to a sort of storeroom. About ten paintings were laid facing towards the wall. 'These were the ones that didn't sell at the last exhibition. Let me see…' He sifted through them. 'Ah yes – Twizel Head, snow and sunset. There we are.'

'It's great. How much do you want for it?'

'Say one hundred and fifty.'

'Pounds or pence.'

'Pounds, I'm afraid. I have to live.'

'Wait until I come into a fortune. Promise you won't sell it to anyone else.'

'I wish I could say yes but I can't. I just live from picture to picture. But I tell you what – here's a little woodcut print of a snow scene. You can have that.'

'But…'

'No – no, if I decide to make a gift, I make a gift and that's it.'

'Thanks – it's lovely. Anyway, I'd better be off.' She went back into the hallway and changed into her wellies, thick coat, scarf and gloves, then put her house shoes into a bag.

Randal followed her to the gate, and put his hand on her shoulder. Clare glanced back at the house and saw Yvette looking at them from a window. She waved. Randal squeezed her shoulder as they said goodbye.

SIXTEEN

Clare got home to find Sheila in one of her moods. She didn't question her; she knew her sister too well for that.

After lunch Sheila went into the yard and stood in the semi-shelter of one of the outhouses. She wanted to think, to be alone, to let yesterday's quarrel seep through her, somehow to mellow it, to let it become a thing of the past. She looked at the garden. That chestnut tree that Clare seemed to have such a feeling about was bare, dead looking, dreary.

But the quarrel. What had caused it? Had anything caused it? Yes. It was that girl who came into the restaurant – she had caused it. She had triggered it off. Everything had been fine until then. Sheila was in a good mood – she thought she was anyway. Nalin likewise – she called him Nalin now, not Dr Vyas as she had at first. The food was fine, no problem there. Even the conversation had been lively, pleasant, up to that point.

And then that girl had come in and sat somewhere behind her at the back of the restaurant. Nalin continued talking to her but he was no longer looking at her. No, he was looking at this unknown girl. Once, twice, three times Sheila looked up and each time his glance was elsewhere. Then she turned her head and looked at this unknown girl. She was young, pretty, fair – a bit like Clare.

Suddenly Sheila felt infuriated. She remembered things, little things from the past. Like that evening after the Dwali play. The same thing. He had been talking to her but all the time looking over her shoulder at Kavita Vora. And even when he had come over to their home, she was sure he had taken more notice of Clare than he had of her. Somehow all this half-forgotten resentment erupted.

What had she said? She could hardly remember. But various things came back to her: 'You only want white girls as prestige symbols'; 'You're only going out with me because I'm the best available'; 'If there were someone younger and prettier, you'd drop me quickly enough'. Things like that.

Sheila regretted it. She caught a glimpse of herself in the cracked mirror hanging in the corner of the out-house. 'My days of youth where are they fled?' – a line from some opera came back to her. And Nalin; he was handsome, successful, fairly well off. Kind, too; Sheila remembered the way he always treated his mother. She had been flattered, so flattered by his attention.

Is it better to live with a lie and be half happy or to face the truth and be wholly miserable? Sheila wasn't sure.

SEVENTEEN

It was just a few days later that Clare ran into Kavita – 'ran into her' almost literally. It happened in the swimming pool. Clare was alone. For a while she sat on the edge watching the way the black lines at the bottom of the pool danced in ever-changing zigzags. It always fascinated her. How she would have loved to paint them. But how could you paint motion like that?

Finally she plunged in. She had only done half a length when – crash! Some object sank to the bottom like a torpedoed warship. Clare was alarmed. 'Oh – are you alright?' she asked, addressing a mass of churning water and dark limbs with no expectation of a reply.

A dark face in a white cap surfaced, eyes tightly shut, mouth spluttering. Then the eyes opened.

'Kavita – it's you. I'm sorry, are you alright?' Clare started laughing – she couldn't stop herself – and Kavita joined in for a moment but then began coughing and spluttering again. 'Here, let me help you out. You must rest for a bit.'

Clare leapt out of the pool and stretched out a hand for Kavita. The two girls rested by the side and then went to the cafeteria for a cup of tea.

Clare wasn't sure what to talk about to Kavita. She didn't really know her; they'd only had that brief, polite conversation after the Dwali play. She said various things that entered her head. One thing puzzled her and she mentioned Sheila's quarrel with Dr Vyas.

A look of distress passed over Kavita's face. How could it be? Clare knew from Miles that Kavita was always ridiculing Dr Vyas so it could hardly be concern for him. As for Sheila, Kavita hardly knew her.

Eventually Kavita became so quiet and serious that Clare asked her if she was alright.

'Yes, yes,' Kavita said. She stretched her hands across the table and took Clare's right hand in both of hers. She smiled. 'I realise I hardly know you but somehow I want to talk. Do you know, I wonder, that feeling when you're terribly happy but that very happiness makes you uncertain, fearful of losing it?'

'Maybe. I don't know that I've experienced it but I can imagine it.'

Kavita released her hand and went back to sipping her tea silently. Clare sensed that she wanted to confide further in her; some sort of inward struggle was going on. But nothing happened and Kavita stayed silent.

As they were going out, Clare put her hand on Kavita's shoulder. 'Remember that I'm your friend. You can come to me. Don't forget, will you?'

'I won't.'

EIGHTEEN

'I have to be at least half a Christian when Christmas comes round,' grumbled Mr Vora every year as the great festival approached.

But Kavita enjoyed Christmas. Admittedly it wasn't quite like the birth of Krishna, which they had celebrated back in September, nor like Dwali. Those two always awakened a thousand memories of her childhood back in Bombay. But Christmas was the one great festival that embraced everyone – Christians, atheists, agnostics, Sikhs, Mohammedans, Hindus. You couldn't escape it. Yes, Kavita liked it: the drifting smell of pine needles as she walked past the florist shops; the endless carols sounding round the piazza. Everyone was happy or, if not happy, at least tried to keep up the appearance of happiness.

For the Vora family, there was another more private festival to follow Christmas: Aditi was getting married early in January. That would leave Kavita as the only unmarried girl in the family. 'We must get a husband for Kavita,' everyone kept saying.

Aditi was the most westernised of the family. Even her looks had something of it: a paler skin and a soft oval face. She was almost as pretty as her youngest sister but less animated. And her lifestyle was western too: she went to the pictures, frequently visited discos and listened to innumerable pop records on the family record player – mainly David Bowie. This annoyed the rest of them, especially Kavita who liked Lata Mangeshkar and all the great Indian singers and performers. No western pop for Kavita.

But when it came to it, Aditi wasn't a rebel. The family decided that she should marry Rohit Shar, a young solicitor's clerk from Birmingham, a friend of a friend. Alright. Aditi shrugged and accepted it. Rohit didn't like David Bowie but apart from that she could find no fault with him. So, while the stylus tracked the groove and sang out 'Love you till Tuesday', the rest of the Vora family fussed over dresses, dowry, hall-booking, catering and a thousand other details that were apparently necessary to this event.

Only Kavita seemed rather apart. She did what was expected of her but nothing more. People noticed things about her at this time, something odd – a sort of fear. As she sat and stitched the red braid in Aditi's white bridal sari, her hands actually trembled. But Kavita had always been a bit strange in her ways. The family made excuses. If she wasn't wildly interested – well, things would just have to go on without her.

And so the preliminaries went ahead: the visit of Rohit's parents to Aditi's home; the giving of money; the placing of the kumkum on Rohit's forehead; the exchanging of gifts. It all was seen to, everything that could contribute to the build up. Kavita participated meekly, palely.

The date of the wedding was fixed for January 10th, the venue Unity Hall. That morning the Vora family were all up early. Everything was still dark, only the street lamps showing through the murkiness. Aditi had her bath; she would have another sacred bath at the ceremony. The fire had gone out and the water was cold. Kavita and Indu had to boil up saucepans on the cooker.

'Why has the fire to go out on my wedding morning?' Aditi shouted, shivering, from the bathroom.

'Don't worry – we'll soon be there.'

Then came the dressing of the bride. Aditi would have to change it all later for the white sari with red braid, but for the journey to the hall there was a yellow sari plus all her garlands and jewellery. Then the coconut to hold in her hands. This detail had been overlooked and Mr Vora hadn't a coconut in the shop. Kavita had to go out to another store that was not officially open and beg for one.

Dr Vyas's car provided Aditi's transport for the few hundred yards to Unity Hall. Kavita was with the party that walked, the chill morning air striking through her thin sari. The hall itself seemed in tune with the dreary morning, its dirty orange walls dotted with posters for long-past events – political meetings, beetle drives, jumble sales. But how bright the saris looked against all this, exotic flowers flaunting the weary January.

At the back of the hall Mr Vora placed the statuette of Ganesh on a table. It was their own Ganesh from home, the Elephant God, the god of beginnings. Cross-legged on the floor they worshipped him and Aditi offered him the coconut. Thank heaven Kavita had managed to beg one. And then Lata and the other young girls threw flower petals over the tiny god.

Aditi now had to take her holy bath and put on the white sari. Kavita helped her find the only bath in the building, a very utilitarian object that only extreme necessity or holiness would have driven anyone to use.

'Heavens, this is rough,' gasped Aditi, glancing at the bare light bulb and the filthy walls.

Kavita smiled one of her more evil smiles and left her sister to get on with it.

'Such a while since I saw you.' Dr Vyas bore down on Kavita as she re-entered the hall. 'When was it? Dwali – after the Dwali play?'

'Yes, I think so. It does seem a long while.'

'And so another of the beautiful Vora sisters is about to be married?'

'It seems so.'

The doctor looked at her inquisitively. Those little black eyes; they could seem laser-like as his glance cut towards you. Then his mother, slow and rheumaticky as ever, approached them. Kavita helped her into a chair.

The doctor looked uncertain, unsure how to carry on the conversation, but Lata saved any embarrassment by running up and begging her auntie to help her re-tie her sari. Soon it was time for Kavita to go back and see if Aditi had finished her holy bath.

Aditi was vigorously rubbing her slim brown body with a tatty discoloured towel when Kavita entered the bathroom. 'Oh, the water was freezing and so is the room. I'm shivering – I'm sure I'll catch cold.'

'Well, if you will get married in January…'

'OK. You make yours in midsummer.'

'I'll find an electric fire.'

Kavita returned with the fire then she went for the white sari with the red braid. She held out the sari and helped to wind it round her sister.

'Where's the mirror?' Aditi asked. 'What – not even a mirror? How do I look then? Tell me.'

Kavita studied her sister. She glanced down at the red braid and for a moment she thought of its significance – the breaking of the hymen, the loss of virginity. The sisters shared a room and confided; at least, Aditi confided in Kavita but not the other way round. Strange really. A fragment of conversation came back to Kavita: Aditi telling her how she had almost made love to a boy after a party but said no at the last moment. Would Rohit have minded? Probably. Anyway.

Kavita banished these thoughts. 'Yes, you look beautiful,' she said.

'What – almost as beautiful as you, I suppose.'

The sisters exchanged smiles, whimsical smiles, but they couldn't have said what they meant. Then they went back to the big hall, the ceremony, the guests.

Thereafter, somehow, Kavita lost interest. It all went ahead, everything fell into its allotted place; no hitch, no problems. The giving of the garlands was lovely really, those yellow garlands and the January rain pattering outside. The chanting of the priest and the exchange of vows; the walking seven times round the fire – yes, it was all performed exactly as everyone wished. But Kavita saw it through a blur. What was it? Weariness? Indifference?

She wasn't sure.

*

Back at home when it was all over, Kavita sat in the bedroom alone. It was now her bedroom, hers only. At one time she had shared this big room with all her four sisters then, starting with Indu, they had all got married from the eldest downwards. In a way she had been looking forward to this moment for years, the time when she would be in full possession, able to do whatever she liked without considering the wishes of the others. All day long she had been anticipating the sensation of selecting her favourite Muni Begum record, setting it on the turntable, lowering the stylus. But when she did so, the descending notes on the sitar, the wandering flute and the haunting voice, seemed not so much beautiful as intensely melancholy.

Kavita lay back on the bed, telling herself that she ought to be happy. But no, she was painfully sad and felt a strange inward loneliness, as if no company – no one at all – could ever relieve it.

One phrase haunted her: 'We must get a husband for Kavita.'

NINETEEN

In the clarity of the early dawn every oak leaf edged with hoar frost shone with a sense of awakening. Tara's breath showed white in the cold air as Clare walked towards the stable carrying the heavy saddle.

She wanted to ride by herself today along the hillside's edge. Alone: she must be alone. She wanted to think.

Tara trod the cold edge of the morning hills. Clare looked vaguely at the low white mist in the wooded valley and the sun climbing above it. But her thoughts weren't really on the morning; she saw instead two faces peering at her through her mind's window: Randal's – sad, hopeful, wondering, and Kavita's – happy, too happy and yet somehow fearful. Fearful of what?

TWENTY

Aditi's wedding had been gone a fortnight. It was Sunday afternoon and Kavita had to serve in the shop. Usually this wasn't expected of her: Mr and Mrs Vora and the elder brothers and sisters did it turn about and Kavita was exempt because she was a student with lots of homework. On this particular afternoon, however, the others were all elsewhere and she had to serve from five until six when Indu would relieve her. But it was well past six and there was no sign of Indu.

This was a crisis. Kavita had to hand in a history essay first thing on Monday morning. The essay wasn't even started; all she had done so far was to memorise the title: 'The Norman Invasion brought England back into the mainstream of European life and led to a rejuvenation of art and culture. Discuss.' Kavita hadn't a clue what the Norman invasion had done for England. Right now, as she banged three tomato soups, half a pound of Cheddar cheese and a packet of Tampax through the check-out, nothing seemed more remote. If only Indu came soon she could make it. She had already realised on Friday that things were desperate and had begged a crib from Sally Gaynor (very clever) and another from Arun Patel.

Then there were the three overdue books from the library on the subject, not looked at yet. If she could only get away now she was sure she could scrape something together ready for Monday. But no – the whole thing had been ruined by Indu. Indu of all people; quite the kindest of her sisters, she treated Kavita more like a daughter than a sister. She hadn't even sent word as to why she was late, despite being only three streets away. And she wasn't on the phone.

So Kavita wearily tapped in some more tomato soup and thought of Miles. Miles – that was it! Miles was good at expressing himself. Of course – he could write that essay for her. She must phone Miles.

Kavita glanced round the shop. There were only three customers and they all seemed engrossed in choosing their purchases. She might just have time. She locked the till, ran to the house and picked up the phone. Oh bother; even as she dialled she glanced through to the shop and saw a customer coming up to the check-out.

'Hello.'

'Oh Miles – I've got a crisis! Can you come?'

'What, now?'

'Yes! Oh heavens – there's another one at the check-out. Can't stop. Bye.'

For the next hour and a half things were busy. There was no sign of Indu – and no sign of Miles.

Miles turned up first. There had been no bus and he had had to walk all the way. He stood to one side of the check-out waiting for Kavita to deal with a customer. He felt irritated by the great pile of groceries that had to take precedence over him. Eventually she was free. 'What's the matter?' he asked.

'Indu hasn't turned up so I've got to manage the shop alone – no one is here to help me. And I haven't started on my history essay, and it's got to be in for tomorrow, first lesson. Mrs Dyson will slaughter me if it's not. Oh please, Miles.' She took his hand. 'Will you write it for me?'

'Um – well. That is – what's it about?'

'The Norman— Oh, those chocolate bars have gone up to eighteen pence – went up on Thursday.' Kavita broke off to address an urchin at the counter.

The child fumbled in his pockets; Kavita was almost tempted to ram the chocolate bar down his throat in annoyance.

'Conquest,' she whispered savagely in Miles' ear.

Miles looked startled and then vague memories of Harold, William the Conqueror and the Battle of Hastings flashed through his mind.

The urchin produced the three extra pennies and grabbed the chocolate bar. At that moment Indu burst into the shop looking fraught. 'It's Lata – the poor child. Sick all day, vomiting into the bucket. Pale as anything. I took her to Dr Smithson and he says it's just stomach upset. Put her to bed, keep her warm – that's all he says. So I put her to bed, keep her warm but still she's sick, sick, sick. Now Mrs Mason from next door has come in – she's looking after her.'

Kavita replied to all this coldly with some details of the till then grabbed Miles' arm and left the shop. 'Did you hear that? Not a word of apology for coming in three hours late. Not a word. Not so much as a "sorry I'm late". And that Lata. I bet she's playing at it. Always pretending she's ill, the spoilt brat.'

Miles didn't reply. He waited until they were in the living room and Kavita had calmed down a bit. 'So, you have a crisis?'

'Yes, I told you. I've got this wretched history essay to do for tomorrow first thing and…'

'But I thought it was some terrible disaster. I've been worrying all the way here.'

'Well, it will be if I don't get the essay written.'

'But it's almost nine o'clock.'

'Have you eaten?'

'No – no.'

'Well, here's the bargain. I cook you a nice meal – for me as well of course – and you write me an essay on the Norman Conquest.'

'I haven't touched the Norman Conquest since I was a small boy.'

'It's alright, I've got two cribs. Here they are. I don't normally do things like this. And here are three library books. You look at them and I'll start on the meal.'

Miles shrugged and looked apprehensively at the three fat volumes. Perhaps the cribs would be a better bet. He read them through as vague fragments of knowledge, gleaned long ago, meandered through his brain: vast gloom-filled cathedrals; peasants working three big fields... The cribs all seemed to agree that the Norman Conquest was a good thing. The only way to avoid the most servile duplication seemed to be to take the other side and to use all the same facts to argue that it was a bad thing.

Filled with the inspiration of desperation, Miles set to work. He lifted sentences at random from the three books and the cribs, reversed their arguments, mixed them up and then glued the whole lot together with memories from his early history lessons. Thus he struggled, like a cook throwing everything into the pot and hoping to God it would add up to a meal.

Meanwhile the actual cook, Kavita, clattered away in the kitchen. Eventually a vegetable pilau steamed its way into the living room. Miles didn't stop but carried on working as he ate.

The meal over, Kavita asked, 'How much longer?'

'About half an hour.'

'I think I'll pop up to Indu's place. Perhaps Lata really is ill. Indu seemed so upset – I was too harsh in my judgement.'

Miles was just finishing the essay when Kavita returned. 'Oh Miles, Lata looks terrible – really awful. I must go back up there and help. And you've finished! How wonderful! Let me read it and then I'll take it to Indu's and copy it out.'

Kavita stood by the mantelpiece reading the essay, her eyes bright with excitement as if it were a masterpiece of historical writing

'That's tremendous,' she gasped. 'I always knew those Normans were a bunch of swine.' She flung her arms around him. 'Oh, I'm so grateful. I give you my soul forever.'

'Only your soul?'

'My soul will have to do for the moment. Now then – what is the time? Ten thirty – you've just time for the last bus if you hurry.'

'But can I—'

'No – no! You've been great already. Those ghastly Normans! I'd have fought for King Harold if I'd been around. Now your coat – let me help you. Look, snowflakes! Just started. Come on.'

She kissed him again in the hallway and Miles reluctantly walked out into the wintry darkness.

*

Kavita gathered her things, her blue biro – essays always looked better in blue – exercise book, ruler, rubber and pencil sharpener, then put on her coat and walked out into the street. The flakes fell phantom-like, lit by the sickly paleness of the sodium lamps. The ground was cold, freezing. Yes, already the snow was settling. Soon it would be thick.

She was soon round at Indu's house.

'You have come back?' asked her sister, with a slight smile of relief.

'Yes.'

'But it's already late.'

'I couldn't forget how sick Lata was looking. Can I come in?'

'Yes, yes – don't stand there. Shake the snow off.'

Indu led the way up to the bedroom. The other two children were asleep. Her husband, Suryakant, was out working; he did shift work.

'We'll watch together,' Indu said.

Kavita sat down and looked at Lata. She did indeed look terrible. Her lovely dark eyes had a look of fear – fear rather than pain.

Kavita drew a small table close to the chair and started copying the essay. Indu sat on the bed holding Lata's hand. For about an hour all was fairly quiet then Lata started to groan. Kavita laid down her pen.

'Indu, I'm sure there's something really serious the matter with Lata. Let me phone the doctor now.'

'But it's late, well after midnight. And besides, Dr Smithson was so unhelpful this afternoon. I'm sure it would be a waste of time.'

'I'll phone Dr Vyas.'

'Dr Vyas?' Indu exclaimed. 'But you're not supposed to trouble other doctors. Besides, I don't think he likes me and he's certainly got little cause to like you after the teasing, sarcastic way you've always treated him.'

A slightly martyred look came into Kavita's eyes. 'I'll phone Dr Vyas,' she repeated.

'As you wish.'

Kavita closed the exercise book, put on her coat and went back out into the snowy street.

TWENTY-ONE

The sound of his mother's embroidery needle weaving in and out irritated Dr Vyas. It was only a little sound, a very little sound, yet it impinged on his world. What a pity not to have a separate study. But no, for the meantime the living room had to do.

His father's portrait hung on the wall beside him. A bearded face, a mystical face. Yes, he had been that sort of person, his nose forever buried in books of learning: the Vedas; the Mahabharata; the Ramayana; the writings of Ghandi and Radhakrishnan and Tagore. His son Nalin respected all that. But somehow…

The embroidery needle continued to annoy him. He got up for a moment, walked over to the window and pulled aside the curtain. Snow was falling and already settling. Down in the valley it looked quite thick. He returned to his book, making a vague murmuring sigh as he did so for no reason that he could have explained.

'You should give up studying at night,' said his mother. 'It will strain your eyes.'

'I'm alright.'

'But why study like this? You've taken all your exams and got high marks. There is no need to study any more.'

'Oh yes, there is. Those fellows who only study for exams and then drop it never get anywhere. I intend to study all my life – and not just what I'm doing at the moment. Background reading too so that I understand medicine as well as I possibly can.'

'And what are you reading?.'

'New perspectives in anal surgery.'

His mother merely groaned at this information and then murmured, 'Just like your father, only with him it was religion and philosophy. Yes, he was a great philosopher.'

Nalin glanced up at his father's picture and, despite himself, an amused smile crossed his lips. Yes, his father knew it all, had read all the books, knew all the theory. But back at home it had been his mother who ruled. She was illiterate – but she ruled. His father was cast merely in the role of an adviser, an adviser whose advice was never taken.

Eventually his mother had had enough of her embroidery. She put the needles back in their box, folded up the bit of cloth and went to bed.

Nalin was relieved to be alone. He resumed his book but he felt restless. His mother's remarks about him being just like his father had irked him. He wanted to be something different, not just a dreamer, something more. And so he sat and thought about his ambitions while vaguely watching the snow fall in big powdery flakes beyond a chink in the curtains.

One a.m. and he was still there. Suddenly the phone rang. Somehow he was pleased, as if this were some challenge he had been waiting for. He picked up the receiver with anticipation. There was a crackle like an icicle breaking, as if winter were trying to speak to him. Then—

'Hello? Kavita Vora here…'

Kavita Vora! If Brahma himself had spoken, Nalin could not have been more surprised.

'Dr Vyas here.'

'Oh, you picked up the phone so quickly you startled me.'

'I was studying late. Can I help you?'

'I do so desperately hope so. It's Lata, my niece. I know you're not her proper doctor…'

'It's alright.'

'She's been sick for the last seven hours and she's getting worse. Dr Smithson says it's only a stomach upset but my sister is so worried – and so am I.'

'I will be there right away'

'But it's snowing hard.'

'I will be there.'

'Oh, you are kind.'

Kavita reminded him of the address – he had been to Indu's house once before – and rang off. Nalin put down the receiver gently, tenderly, reverently.

*

Nalin went out. Somewhere, far beyond the snow and the clouds that bore it, he saw the moon – the half moon – lying on its back, low in the sky, soft and beautiful. But his thoughts were not on such things. He looked at the hill that led steeply from his house down into Holmefield. It was all snow and there might be ice underneath. He must be careful.

He got in the car and drove slowly down the long hill then along Grimshaw Street towards Indu's home. The front door was clogged with drifting snow. Indu opened it. 'This way.'

He went upstairs and entered the bedroom. Lata was lying diagonally across the bed in a red dressing gown, her head resting in Kavita's lap. Kavita looked up as he came in but did not smile.

Dr Vyas went across to the bed to check the symptoms. At that moment they heard someone else coming in the door and up the stairs. Mrs Vora came into the bedroom and stood at the bottom of the bed. Dr Vyas looked at her.

The prematurely wrinkled features smiled at him, the sort of welcoming smile he had hoped to get from Kavita but hadn't. Mrs Vora stood there for a moment looking at them, Kavita with Lata's head in her lap and the doctor bending over the child. Had Mrs Vora been a Christian, she might have seen it as a Madonna and Child with St Joseph, or perhaps Elijah raising the dead child. As it was, she looked as if she saw something, something significant. The pause only lasted a moment, a tiny action of time. Then a groan from Lata awoke them to a sense of urgency.

'The symptoms? Right – what are they?' Dr Vyas rattled out his question to Indu.

'Pain, sickness, constipation.'

'Pain – but where?'

'Here,' Indu pointed to below the child's stomach. 'But now she says it's moved to here.'

Lata moved her right hand and pressed it to her side. 'The pain is there now?' Dr Vyas asked. Lata nodded. 'Appendicitis.'

'So Dr Smithson was wrong,' Mrs Vora half-screamed.

'Of course – the silly old fool.'

A smile like a secret code passed between the doctor and Mrs Vora.

'We must get her to hospital at once – an operation. Miss Vora,' he turned to Kavita, 'please phone 22233. Tell them it's an emergency. Don't ask for an ambulance, we will go in my car. Appendectomy required. Child of…?'

'Six.'

'We'll be there in ten minutes.'

'No, I will phone,' broke in Mrs Vora. Then to Kavita: 'You go in the car and help with Lata.'

Mrs Vora went off along the snowy pavement to the phone box while the two sisters carried Lata and laid her on the back seat. Kavita sat on Indu's lap in the passenger seat, both mother and aunt turning to watch over Lata.

The child was in acute pain and started to scream. Dr Vyas looked tense, even more so when the car wheels started to skid on the long hill up to the infirmary. But somehow it regained its grip and they arrived safely.

*

They left Lata and her mother at the emergency ward then Nalin drove Kavita back to her home. As the car drew up Kavita turned to him. 'Dr Vyas, I must thank you most sincerely on behalf of the whole family for what you have done tonight.' When she finished, she gave him a look – her lips and her eyes moved very slightly. Was it a smile? He wasn't sure.

'I merely did my duty, Miss Vora.'

Kavita got out without another word.

*

As he finally drove back up the hill, he noticed the half-moon still there beneath the snow clouds, serene, beautiful.

'Kavita – poetry – Kavita,' he murmured to himself.

TWENTY-TWO

After she got out of Dr Vyas's car, Kavita went into the shed, got the front-door key from under the flowerpot and entered the house. 'What a night,' she murmured.

And it was then that she remembered her history essay, still only half-copied, and lying on the table in Lata's bedroom. Should she bother? She was in a state that had passed beyond weariness. But no; after going through so much that night she wasn't going to be defeated.

Back she went into the street round to Indu's house once more. Fortunately they had departed in such a panic that one of the sash-cord windows had been left open. Kavita pulled it up and clambered cautiously over a sill of pot plants and onto the floor. She tiptoed upstairs. Malti and Kishore were asleep in their room; she must remember to send someone round in the morning to look after them. Then she grabbed her exercise book and went back home. There she made some coffee to keep herself awake and sat up in bed copying out the essay.

It was seven o'clock before it was finished. She read it through with relief. Then breakfast and the bus to college. She handed the essay to Mrs Dyson at once; that morning was the absolute deadline. Mrs Dyson said nothing yet the quick tug she gave as she took it from Kavita's hands seemed to express 'and about time too'.

'God, if only you knew the trouble I've gone to for that thing,' Kavita muttered as she went back down the corridor.

*

And then on Wednesday afternoon, suddenly things seemed to start getting better. History was first thing, and Kavita found her attention riveted by the story of Hereward the Wake.

At the end of the lesson Mrs Dyson handed back the homework essays. 'By Christ, she marked those quickly,' whispered Sally Gaynor, who usually got top marks. But the oddest thing was that Mrs Dyson actually smiled as she handed Kavita her work. How strange!

Kavita didn't bother to check what mark she had got. She was in a hurry. The rest of the afternoon was free and it was visiting time at the infirmary. She must get there in time and see how Lata was getting on.

Holmefield Infirmary was only three hundred yards or so from the college. Kavita walked – or rather ran – and arrived at Ward Seven quite breathless. Indu was already at Lata's bedside. As soon as she saw Kavita coming in, she jumped up and embraced her warmly. Indu was always affectionate to Kavita but there was something special about that embrace.

Kavita turned to look at Lata, and realised how much better the little girl was. Happiness had come back into her eyes. And Kavita basked in the thought that she was the heroine of Sunday night. She had guessed that Lata had something worse than a stomach upset; she had broken through the bureaucracy, contacted Dr Vyas, and they had got Lata to hospital just in time. A bit later and Lata would have had a burst appendix. That would have been really serious.

Kavita came out of the hospital alone, feeling jubilant. She stood for a moment in the car park. Workmen were busy clearing snow in the bright wintery sunlight. Then she remembered the history essay, reached for her satchel, pulled out the exercise book and looked at the last page of the essay: 'A – Excellent work. A most original standpoint. Nicely expressed too. You are starting to do yourself justice – well done!'

Kavita laughed aloud and spontaneously broke into a few steps of Indian dance. Was anyone watching? She glanced round. No.

She felt a wild urge to go and show it to Miles, to share the joke, to share her sudden happiness. She knew that he had the whole of the afternoon free. Right now he would be up at the vicarage at Tostenland. She pictured him (or tried to) in his room drawing a snow scene out of the window. But Kavita had never actually been to Tostenland – never seen the vicarage, never met Miles' parents. She suspected he was a bit shy of taking her there. She wondered if his parents would be prejudiced against her; she wasn't sure. But at that moment all other considerations seemed unimportant compared with her wish to show Mrs Dyson's remarks to Miles.

She went back home and changed into her cerise sari, the one she had worn for the Dwali play. This was odd: Kavita didn't normally wear anything so exotic during the day but somehow she wanted to look thoroughly Indian. That was how Miles' parents had to see her.

She took the bus, which went to Tostenland by a highly circuitous route. She almost clapped her hands as it rounded the top of the big hill above Holmefield and a landscape of little fields and woods opened out beyond, with the spire of Tostenland Church in the background. How lovely it looked, the low winter sun catching the stalks of the stubble fields.

Only as she walked up to the front door did Kavita feel the slightest sense of nervousness and hesitation. It was the angelic boy carved on the keystone who did it. He seemed to be looking at her, weighing her up. She looked for the bell. Ah yes. But it wasn't a normal electric push-bell, it was an old-fashioned pull-bell. A deep 'dong' sounded.

Suddenly Kavita felt a fit of the giggles coming on. She looked away, looked at the faded red flowers of a hydrangea in the front garden. She was sure there was still a look of frivolity on her face as she turned back and looked into the cool blue eyes of a middle-aged woman. The eyes registered surprise as she took in the unexpected image of the Indian girl in the vivid sari.

'I'm Kavita,' she said simply.

'Kavita – oh yes! We've heard a lot about you – but I suppose that's a silly thing to say.'

Kavita stepped inside. The hall seemed dark, gloomy. A door opened and a man in a dog collar appeared, obviously the vicar. Strangely handsome, Kavita thought.

'This is Kavita,' said the blue-eyed woman.

'Kavita – what a lovely name. You are a poem.'

Kavita laughed. 'I am but how do you know?'

'Out in India for many years, as a missionary.'

'I see. Where's Miles?'

'Up in his room. I'll fetch him.'

'D'you mind if I step back into the garden for a few moments while I wait? It looks so beautiful.'

Kavita was beside a variegated holly out of sight of the house when Miles ran to her. They embraced and Kavita released the giggles she had been bottling up for the last few minutes.

'Whatever's the matter with you?' Miles asked, almost alarmed.

'Oh, I just had to give way to that! But here – see, look at this and you'll have to laugh as well.' She opened her exercise book and showed him Mrs Dyson's remarks. They laughed together, embraced, laughed again. They were like a couple of little kids. Then Kavita glanced round the garden and looked at the view beyond. 'Where's Clare's house?' she asked.

'It's that one over there on the very edge of the village. See? Beyond the stables. It used to be a farmhouse.'

'Oh yes.' She kissed him again. 'I wonder what your mother thinks of me? I had this fit of laughter as I stood at the door. I'm sure there was a smirk on my face when I looked round at her. She'll think I'm crazy.'

'Never mind. Let's go in again.'

When they got back indoors, Miles' mother asked Kavita to stay for the evening meal. For the rest of the afternoon Miles showed Kavita some of his paintings and drawings then they went for a short walk towards Clare's house.

*

Miles had feared that the evening meal would be awkward but he needn't have worried. His normally austere stepfather mellowed as he questioned Kavita about her home back in India. She mentioned Poona. Yes, he remembered Poona. From there the conversation took off. Memories of places were swopped in a ceaseless flow, with Miles and his mother quite excluded. What little reserve Kavita had was quite forgotten. From places she went on to people, to traditions, to song, to dancing.

'And could we see one of your dances?' asked the Vicar enthusiastically.

'Of course! I will do the one about Krishna stealing the milkmaid's clothes.'

'But what will you do for music?' put in Miles.

'I've a cassette in my handbag. I always carry a cassette of my dance music. Have you a player?'

'Yes – yes.'

'Your young lady is prepared for everything,' said the vicar, smiling benignly at his stepson.

The dirty dishes were hastily stacked in the kitchen, the big table and chairs pushed into a corner, and Kavita took up her position in the centre of the room, the light from the fire shimmering on the folds of her sari.

Miles couldn't quite believe it. Was he really about to see Kavita dancing in the vicarage drawing room? And that dance of all dances! Why, it was so outrageous – not the dance itself but the legend it portrayed.

Kavita stood still for a moment, her hands clasped in front as she gave a somewhat bowdlerised version of the legend. 'This is the story of how Lord Krishna as a young boy found some milkmaids bathing in the river, ran off with their clothes and climbed a tree.'

Kavita slipped off her shoes and stood on tiptoe for a moment then the dance evolved and emerged, not wildly but with a sort of slow, enthralling excitement. It wasn't just her body that moved, it was her hands and her eyes too – everything – they all had meaning, a meaning that flowed out from her dark pupils and through the tips of each slender finger. The room seemed no longer the vicarage drawing room; no, that existence was years ago. Right now some new message about life and the nature of life, some message that had lain as dry seed from the earliest time, was being acted out and displayed in all its exotic beauty.

Coldly, from the shadowed mantelpiece, the sad eyes of a dying god looked down from a cross. Strangely, the Virgin stared out from a print of Raphael's Sistine Madonna as if in beautiful bewilderment at these puzzling patterns of death and rebirth. For one instant Kavita glanced at Miles, the edges of her mouth puckered, and then the dance ended quietly. Kavita stood and held her hands together in a namaste gesture.

That was the climax of the evening. What followed was only desultory conversation and later Miles took Kavita back to the village bus shelter. The evening had passed so happily but, as they stood there, Miles noticed a curiously troubled look on Kavita's face. He tried to cheer her. 'Well, you certainly won over my parents,' he said.

'Your stepfather, yes. Your mother – I'm not so sure.'

'But even so, why are you looking sad?'

'I've remembered something from Sunday night – something I'd half forgotten. I told you about Lata being rushed to hospital and all that but there was one thing I didn't tell you – something I did that I'd sooner not have had to.'

'Something wrong, you mean?'

'No, not wrong. Just a compromise that I fear I may have to pay for.'

'How do you mean pay for?'

But at that moment the bus loomed and slushed its way through the snow to the shelter. Kavita jumped on quickly as if wishing to avoid further conversation. She sat down and waved at Miles, sadly, miserably. The gaiety of the evening seemed to have suddenly gone.

TWENTY-THREE

It was later that week when something happened to Yvette that puzzled her. Only trivial, of course – but strange.

Yes, it was on the Wednesday. She and Clare had gone swimming. There was quite a bond between Clare and Yvette now; they'd somehow taken to each other. Little things had led to it, such as them both liking Joan Baez. The two of them were undressing in the changing room when Yvette noticed a reddish mark on Clare's shoulder. Only slight but distinctive.

'What's that?' Yvette asked.

Clare blushed, laughed and then said, 'Oh, someone got carried away a bit.'

For no apparent reason, she kissed Yvette on the forehead. Yvette filed the incident away in her mind as one of those unexplained mysteries which life occasionally produces. But on the Saturday something happened that explained it.

She had gone to the pictures with Simon, her new boyfriend. Afterwards he had taken her up one of the quaint old back yards that were a feature of Holmefield. Simon wanted to fondle her breasts. She'd never let a boy do that before but yes – why not? Then there was a fumbling around with her bra and jumper – all a bit awkward. It was a cold night as well.

Unfortunately, when they got to the bus garage she realised that the ten o'clock bus up the valley had already gone. She'd have to wait for the one at eleven and that would mean being really late – and there was a two-mile walk from the last bus stop to her home to think about.

It was one a.m. before Yvette finally reached the house. She felt tired and slightly guilty. Her father had been out with Clare that evening but he had obviously returned to the house much earlier; she could see the fresh tyre marks were already filling up with drifting snow.

As soon as she went into the hallway Yvette sensed that something was different. What? She couldn't define it. Everything was in its usual place; there was nothing new or unexpected. And yet the atmosphere was strange – but nice, somehow. And the feeling of guilt and tiredness seemed to leave her.

She went into the kitchen, brewed up some tea then came back into the hallway to try to define that strange something. Perfume! That was it. The tiniest smell of perfume. She realised there was a note lying on the hall table in her father's large curving hand:

Dearest Yvette,

Tonight I am sleeping with Clare. Hope you'll understand.

Love Dad

Yvette looked up the stairs at the door of her father's bedroom. Beyond that door her father and Clare would be lying together in the big bed with the blue coverlet, sleeping in each other's arms. Yvette felt a great love for Clare and for her father too. She stretched her hands up in the direction of the door, a strange gesture, almost as if she were blessing them.

TWENTY-FOUR

It was a grey day, grey and snowy. Kavita was worried as she sat at her desk at college, the big flakes coming down beyond the window. It was history again but her attention was totally elsewhere. It was that brief sight yesterday as she had returned home in the late evening from Aditi's; even from a hundred yards away there was no mistaking Dr Vyas's mother coming out of Wesley Street. What on earth could she have gone down to Wesley Street for except...

But what was she worrying about? Seeing an old lady emerging from Wesley Street. Was that so terrible? There were a thousand reasons why Mrs Vyas might have been in Wesley Street. Perhaps she was visiting someone; maybe she had gone to the shop to buy something. But an old lady like that, bad on her legs, going all the way to Wesley Street with the snow only just cleared off the pavement by the road sweepers? Yes – she must have had a very strong motive.

When Kavita saw Mrs Vyas, all the fears of the last six months rushed in on her. She was so shocked that she didn't go straight home but walked round the block three times. When she finally got back, her parents were already in bed.

What would happen this evening? That would be the proof. She almost longed to get home to fulfil her worst fears – or else prove them unfounded.

It was Indu who opened the door. One glance at her face and Kavita was certain that things were exactly as she feared. It was difficult to say exactly how Indu looked; she had a sort of blank fearing expression.

'Everything alright?' Kavita asked, addressing the look rather than anything Indu had said. Indu merely shrugged. 'Lata OK?'

'Yes, she'll be home tomorrow. She's recovered quickly thanks to Dr Vyas.'

'Yes, thanks to Dr Vyas,' Kavita repeated with an acid tone in her voice.

'Please, please Kavita – be reasonable.' Indu put a hand on her sister's shoulder.

'Reasonable about what?'

'You'll find out.'

'No doubt. I think I already know.'

A memory of Sunday night passed through her mind. Kavita suddenly jerked Indu's hand from her shoulder and gave her a sharp, malevolent look. But why treat her favourite sister like that? She wasn't sure.

Nothing significant was said over the evening meal; in fact, very little was said at all. Kavita suddenly felt how quiet the house was since Aditi's wedding. She was the last sister. Trapped. Yet there she was, as ever, with Indu and her parents. They all loved her; what was there to fear? But the house – it was so silent.

'Kavita, we wish to speak to you,' said her father as soon as the meal was over.

'I know.'

'How do you know?'

'I know a lot of things.'

'We are lucky to have such a clever daughter.' Mr Vora intended this as a bit of light-hearted raillery but it didn't come off.

Kavita looked at her father. She didn't smile. It struck her how old he looked, how old both her parents looked. They could have been her grandparents; there was ample space for another generation in between.

Indu started taking the dirty dishes into the kitchen. Kavita regretted that hostile look of earlier on. She wanted Indu to stay in the room and support her. She grabbed her sister's hand, pressed it. She thought Indu would get the message but Indu pulled her hand away and continued clearing the table. Then she went into the kitchen to do the washing-up and shut the door.

Mr and Mrs Vora sat down on the sofa together. Kavita took up a half-kneeling position on the easy chair, her hands gripping the sides, like a cornered tigress about to spring.

'Sit down properly and listen to what we say,' said Mr Vora.

Kavita modified her position slightly.

'Right. Well, Kavita, we have been thinking – planning— That is to say we've been...' Mr Vora seemed to have lost track of what he was going to say.

His wife butted in. 'To be brief, we have arranged a marriage between you and Dr Vyas. It will be announced right away and the actual marriage will take place in late summer when you finish college.'

Kavita said nothing. Her only response was to go back to her tigress-like position.

Mr Vora fidgeted around. 'Well, surely you've got something to say.'

Kavita leant forward slightly and said in a quiet hiss, 'I say no.'

'And we say yes – and that's that,' cut in Mrs Vora.

Mr Vora glanced at Kavita. Her look of determined hatred quite shocked him. 'Now, now – let's hear what Kavita has to say,' he put in. 'She may have objections we can resolve.'

'So I suppose this is what that old woman came to see you about yesterday.'

'Mrs Vyas?' asked her father. 'Why yes. But we had been hoping that something like this would work out for some while.'

'And what about me? Are my feelings about the matter of any interest to you? Let me tell you— Let me think about my first impression of Dr Vyas. It was at that party round about Dwali, not this year – last. Dr Vyas was there with Sheila Field. You know, Clare's sister. I only just knew him. Anyway, all the time he was talking to Sheila he was glancing over her shoulder at me. I didn't encourage him, not one little bit. But as his eyes caught mine for one second it was as if I saw a warning light like a lighthouse showing up dangerous rocks. I said to myself, "Beware of that man. If you let him, he will bring trouble into your life." And from then on I never missed an opportunity to be offhand with him – to be rude, and scornful. It wasn't my nature, mind, but it seemed that the more I was unpleasant to him, the more he noticed me. And when I heard he had broken with Sheila Field I knew—'

'Rubbish! All this is ridiculous,' broke in her mother. 'Think what is being offered. This man is handsome, he is highly intelligent, he has a good job, he is always neatly dressed, he is kind to his moth—'

'Oh for heaven's sake,' Kavita shouted, half-springing from the chair. 'I don't care if he's been tailor-made by Lord Brahma—'

'Sit down! Sit down in that chair properly and let's look at this in a sensible way,' broke in her father.

Kavita sat on the chair, crossed one leg over the other, rested her head back and folded her hands in her lap. It was a pose of mock subservience. And then the whole thing suddenly struck her as funny; her mouth wanted to twitch into a mocking smile.

'I suppose,' resumed her father more calmly, 'it's the question of age. You are nineteen and Nalin is twenty-seven – eight years older. It must seem a long time. But when he is fifty-eight and you are fifty it will be quite unimportant.'

A hollow laugh was Kavita's only reply.

'And besides, remember last Sunday night? Think of what Dr Vyas did for Lata – saved her life probably...'

'All right, all right – I am grateful. But what I did that night was for Lata's sake – nothing else. I knew full well I was making use of his interest in me in order to get something done for Lata. So OK, I handed him a blank cheque. But isn't it cruel for him to cash it so soon – and for such a sum? This is my whole life he is asking—'

'Why on earth can't you be like Aditi?' muttered her mother. 'We thought she would be a rebel – all that listening to pop songs and such like. But when we arranged the marriage with Rohit, she did what she was told and that was that.'

'Aditi is Aditi and I'm me. That's the difference.'

'Yes. You were the youngest. We spoilt you. I can see our mistake now.'

But Kavita wasn't listening to her mother; she was looking at her father. His features were gentler and, acting on impulse, Kavita suddenly felt she might gain advantage by a more emotional approach. She knelt on the carpet in front of him and took his hands in hers.

'Father, over and above all this – I mean my real reason – is that I love someone else.'

'Love, love, love,' muttered Mrs Vora derisively but Kavita ignored her.

Continuing to address her father, she continued. 'I love Miles and he loves me. We want to get married. Can't you understand? Isn't that simple enough?'

Her father looked uncomfortable, embarrassed. He shrugged his shoulders, sighed slightly. Kavita looked at her mother, whose eyes had the look of one who sees an easy victory transformed into a humiliating defeat.

Abruptly Mrs Vora stood up. 'This argument is getting nowhere. We are just going round in circles. Let's leave it for tonight. But–' she pointed towards Kavita '–if you won't listen to reason, we will have to use sterner measures. Do you hear?'

TWENTY-FIVE

Next day at college, the previous evening's quarrel seemed somehow remote. Kavita sat there during the first lesson, glancing at the other girls. She knew the secrets of several of them from conversations in the girls' toilets, things like that. Most of them were on the Pill and several were living with their boyfriends. Her own dilemma – was it real?

But as the morning progressed, the memories of what had happened came back to her. She dwelt on little things she had only half noticed at the time. Indu's attitude, for example – the way she had just gone into the kitchen and shut the door. After all that Kavita had done for Indu on that Sunday night— Yes, and it was largely that which had triggered off this crisis. She remembered the warm affectionate embrace Indu had given her in the hospital ward. Yet only a few days later she had deserted Kavita, left her to face her parents' pressure alone. She might have stayed in the room, put in the odd word of support. But no.

And then she remembered her mother's remark at the very end of the argument: 'If you won't listen to reason, we will have to use sterner measures.' What measures? Were they going to subject her to a water torture every night? In view of the indulgent, loving way her parents had always treated her it seemed highly unlikely.

Eventually Kavita persuaded herself that they would probably let the matter rest for a bit – a month perhaps, in the hope that she would change her mind. Not that she would, of course, but it would give her time to gather strength, make plans, talk it over with people. And who would she confide in? Not Indu – no, not after last night. Miles, of course; that was obvious. Vaguely she felt embarrassed; in the heat of yesterday's argument, she had exaggerated their relationship. Marriage hadn't been mentioned, not so much as the word. Yet somehow, to maintain her present strength it was necessary to believe that it had been. But she felt she needed someone more apart from the situation as well, more objective.

Suddenly Clare flashed into her mind. Clare! Yes, of course. And she remembered the conversation at the swimming pool.

There were no lessons that afternoon. Kavita almost wished there were for she dreaded going home. When it came to lunchtime, she had half a mind to go and seek out Miles, wherever he might be. But no. She decided to go home and find out how her parents had decided to treat her.

But the first look at her parents' faces removed all hope of a month's respite. Lunch went by without the subject being mentioned but in countless little ways she was made uncomfortable. Her parents seemed to be putting on an act of heroic patience. Should she react with anger or just laugh at them? She suspected that if only there had been someone to laugh with, she would have chosen the latter course. But there was no one.

How hard to be the youngest child! Spoilt in childhood, loaded with all the nothingness, the trivia, and then at the approach of adulthood to have all the half-frustrated expectations of ageing parents loaded on her. How cruel! How absurd!

Kavita finished the meal and took her satchel up to her bedroom. She thought she would stay there for a while and do her homework; it would be a temporary sanctuary. But she didn't start at once. Instead she sat on the bed and looked through the window, beyond the dark streets and mill chimneys, to where the insipid January sunlight was playing on the white, wide curves of the snowy moorland.

She was surprised by a knock on the door. 'Come in.'

Her mother entered. She came and sat on the bed but at a distance. 'Kavita, we will give you one more chance. Will you agree to marry Dr Vyas?'

'I thought we went through all that yesterday. You don't think I'd change my mind about a thing like that overnight, do you?'

'I see,' was all her mother said. She got up from the bed, went out of the door and shut it. Then Kavita heard the sound of the lock turning.

'What are you doing?' she shouted, running to the door. 'What on earth are you doing?' She banged on the door, turned the handle. 'What are you doing?' she repeated.

'Making you come to your senses. You will stay there until you agree to our wishes.'

'But that's absurd! People only do things like that in silly novels.'

'Well you shouldn't act like a character in a silly novel then.'

'But what happens when I want to go to the loo?'

'There's a chamber pot under the bed.'

'That won't last for ever.'

'You'd better make up your mind quickly, then.'

'And eating – how do I eat? And what about college tomorrow...' But her mother's footsteps could already be heard descending the stairs.

Kavita went back and sat on the bed. She felt like a character in a play – a pantomime or a fairy story. So, she was a prisoner in her own room. Right; might as well pretend to take it seriously. And really it was serious. Her parents, usually so doting and loving, had actually done this to her. Yes, it was serious – but it was also utterly ludicrous. And what could be the dénouement to this little comedy? What would people think when she didn't turn up for college? Something was bound to happen. But what?

She was a prisoner. Better take stock of things. What resources were there? First she inspected the chamber pot. Yes, sure enough there it was. She pulled it out and read the legend 'Ewart 1873' inscribed beneath a coat of arms. Vaguely she wondered if it were really that old but that didn't seem to have much bearing on her dilemma. The next thing was food. Yes, that was lucky; she had bought three bars of her favourite chocolate on the way home –it was a type her father didn't sell. And there was an uneaten apple in her satchel, a trifle rotten but never mind. What about entertainment? All those records were under the gramophone, much played but they would stand another hearing. As for books, there were plenty. Kavita began to think that it was going to be rather fun being a prisoner.

And then she thought of the greatest pleasure of all. She opened the wardrobe and there were all her clothes:

saris, salwars, kurtas, in so many beautiful colours. Yes, soon she would try them all on, every one. And with her favourite sari on, the cerise one, she would add her gold bracelets and bangles, put on a record and do her whole repertoire of dances. Curtains pulled, light on the mirror turned to show the effect. Yes, being a prisoner was going to be fun.

But first there was another thing to think of: escape. She was sure that every prisoner checked on an escape route if there was one. The room had no skylight and the door was locked. That just left the window.

Kavita went across to it and looked out. It was no use; it faced on to the back yard and below was a spiked iron fence. Useless to jump – too much risk of being impaled. Kavita loved life and she had no wish to lose it either by intent or accident.

Could she call for help? Through a gap in the houses she could see some workmen in the next street. Right now they were gathered round a brazier drinking tea. A warm brazier and tea! That was the main thing lacking in her prison: a fire. The electric fire that she sometimes brought upstairs on cold evenings was down in the living room, irretrievable. Never mind.

Kavita shut the window tightly to conserve the heat. Then she did as she had intended, trying on all her clothes. When she was finally wearing the cerise sari, she went through all her dances, watching herself in the mirror, both performer and audience.

Kavita was not without vanity and she smiled back at her own beauty often. 'And so this is what is being offered to Dr Vyas, is it?' In her mind she pictured him looking at her down his microscope like an interesting specimen of bacteria. And she wanted to smash that microscope, smash everything that looked at her coldly, objectively.

She thought of Miles, her shy boy. Yes, she would give it all to Miles. She suddenly felt a strange, painful spasm of love, the will to give herself – every atom of beauty, every spark of devotion.

Eventually the dancing tired her. She sank back on the bed. What to do now? Homework? Yes – why not? Life must go on.

She placed a pillow in a comfortable position, rested back her head and scattered her textbooks over the bed. She read the title for the next essay: 'How did William consolidate his conquest of England?' A fortnight to complete it. She was in good time. No distractions.

Kavita lay back, and picked up the fattest of the textbooks. Why not do this one really thoroughly? She almost rejoiced at the length of the chapter on William's reign.

The military conquest of England was only the first part of William's strategy. No sooner was it accomplished than he set about...

*

Kavita woke up. Her first impression was that she was cold, very cold. And there was something pressing on her lap. Of course, the heavy textbook she had fallen asleep over. And then— Something was wrong. She was unhappy. What was it? It all came back: the conflict with her parents; the quarrel; the key turning in the lock. Now it didn't seem at all funny.

It was cold, so terribly cold. And she felt lonely. No one to talk to. If only she wasn't so cold. The fire, the electric fire, downstairs.

What to do?

She went to the window. The lights shone back from the empty streets, the vague sick yellow of sodium lamps. Horrid! But there was one light that was different – warm, red, comforting. The workman's brazier was still burning How lovely it would be to go up to it to warm her hands. But how to get there?

The oldest trick of all suddenly occurred to her: make a rope of the curtains. Easy; she had seen it once on a film. How stupid not to have thought of it before.

Kavita wrapped herself up in all the warm clothing she could find then she took down the curtains, tied them together and attached one end to the leg of the heavy wardrobe. She climbed out of the window and slid gently down the wall. Some ivy helped her. She was surprised how easy it was; there was no risk of falling on the spiked iron fence.

She went out through the gate and along a cobbled snicket to the next street. The brazier burned by itself; there was no one near. She went across to it and stretched out her hands. Warmth, lovely warmth. Like kindness from a stranger, it soaked into her, comforted, reassured. And it was so beautiful being there by herself. Yet how odd! Everything had gone strange since yesterday. Here she was, warming her hands at a brazier in the middle of the night as if it were normal. The time? The clock on the church struck two a. m.

A noise. Kavita started and turned round. A man, about fifty yards away, coming towards her. He lurched, zigzagging across the pavement, drunk. What should she do? Perhaps he was harmless.

Fear of the cold and fear of the drunk tugged at her. She stood up and moved away; her pace quickened. She turned. The drunk had taken her place by the fire. No need to fear him – but she envied him. He had that lovely fire. He had also cut off her route back home. Not that it was home; no, it had become a prison, somewhere cold, somewhere terrible.

She walked on. The moon was full and it was amazing what she could see. The tall dark mill chimneys stretching up against the moon's luminosity. The little streets, black against the half-melted snow in the gardens. The moors – yes, she could see the moors, white, ethereal, like some great Himalayan abode of snow beyond the town. Beautiful. Comforting.

The moors, the hills. Miles. Clare. Should she go to Miles? No, his parents – well, his mother – that was the problem.

But Clare? That would be different. Clare, the fairy godmother sort of person. Yes, she would go to Clare. But where did Clare live? In a farmhouse about a mile from Tostenland vicarage – but where was that? Kavita's sense of direction was poor. But those hills were the foothills of the moors and there were the moors ahead of her. So she must make for the moors.

Her wanderings now became purposeful as if she had arranged it all and Clare would be expecting her. Going to Clare was uppermost in her mind. She thought of home; in the morning her parents would see the curtains dangling from the window and realise she had gone. They would be alarmed. Questions would be asked which would require answers. What about college? Her non-appearance would need to be explained and her parents would suffer. She wanted them to suffer. She loved her parents and knew they had acted against their inclinations but still – they had locked her in her room. Yes, they must suffer.

And so she was glad, glad to be leaving home. Every step was a step further, every step a stab of revenge at her parents.

And Clare? Clare was somewhere ahead in that farmhouse near the end of the moorland. She was waiting, waiting. She would help Kavita, comfort her, advise her…

Kavita came to a track that branched off the main road to the right. It seemed to promise to take her away from the town. She glanced at the moon hanging full in the cloudless sky as if asking advice from the mythical man that lived there.

And so she moved on to the track. To the moors, to Clare.

TWENTY-SIX

Yvette watched her father's Land Rover go out of the gate, the headlights catching the heavily falling snow as it swung out into the road. She felt bitter. He was going to meet Clare and they would be having a meal together. It wasn't that she was jealous of Clare; no, nothing like that. In fact, she loved Clare – any other word would be an understatement. It was just that she, Yvette, was excluded.

Her father had mentioned it earlier in the day. 'Yvette–' (significantly he usually just said 'dear') '– Yvette, I'm taking Clare out for a meal this evening.'

'Oh good. Can I come too?'

A slightly pained look crossed her father's face. 'Well, no, I'd sooner you didn't. It's not often that I have a chance to be alone with Clare.'

'Why? You're forever alone with her.'

'This is different. It's special.'

Yvette flushed with anger but didn't reply. But when her father shouted goodbye as he left, she ignored him. She wanted to inflict that tiny drop of pain to curdle the evening's pleasure.

And now she pictured them together. They had probably gone to The Pheasant, one of the poshest restaurants in the area. Normally her father wouldn't have been able to afford it but recently he had sold several pictures in quick succession, at good prices too. And this evening would be the very pinnacle of his pleasure.

Just to be there in that luxurious setting – thick carpets, shiny brass ornaments, tank of tropical fish illuminated in one corner, real log fire roaring up the chimney. And then to have Clare with him, a girl half his age and beautiful. Yes, Clare was beautiful. Her father loved beauty and feminine beauty most of all.

Clare would probably be wearing her green dress. Blue suited her better but green would be fine; she didn't like hot colours. Her long fair hair would swoop from her forehead over her shoulders down to her waist. Tonight her father, normally so casual, had put on his best suit and a clean white shirt. How finely his well-tanned skin contrasted with that snow-white shirt.

No doubt he would be full of himself; Clare's company would ensure that. He would ask for a cigar, then the wine list and select with care. Next, the menu. Quiet discussion over the choice of food. Clare leans forward and a strand of her hair rests against Yvette's father's hand. He pretends not to notice but it is more intoxicating than any wine. And then the food; lots of delicious food.

All right, good for them. Why not enjoy themselves? Her father worked hard; he was a man of talent. It was his right. But why couldn't she, Yvette, be there? She would have liked to share their happiness. Instead of which here she was, shut up in this house miles from anywhere with nothing to do.

Or at least not really nothing. Yvette wasn't easily bored – she always found something. For a while she stood at the landing window watching the lights of her father's vehicle dimming slowly as he wove his way down the windy road through the snow-covered side valley. A long road. She could still see him two miles away. And she regretted slightly not saying goodnight. What would it have cost her? Two little words for her to utter and the omitting of a trivial revenge.

But no, they had missed her out.

The lights of the Land Rover finally disappeared but Yvette continued standing there. The snow was still falling slowly most of the time but with sudden flurries. Starting to lie deep too; it was the worst storm of the whole winter so far. How would her father get home? And there was a wind, the east wind, the cold one. She could see it tugging at the weathervane down in the yard. And high above, glimpsed through the whirling snow, was the moon. Yes, the moon at the very peak of its fullness going behind rugged clouds for a moment then reappearing suddenly, bright, triumphant.

Yvette fell into a reverie watching it. Her mind wandered to poetry. The moon and poetry – they were linked. She loved poetry, especially sad romantic poems about 'old, unhappy, far-off things'. Ballads like 'Mary Hamilton', that sort of thing. She went downstairs and pulled a collection of longer poems from the bookcase. Then she sat by the fire and started to read:

'Tis the middle of night by the castle clock,
And the owls have awakened the crowing cock…'

The mood wrapped round her, the mood, the poetry, the firelight. In the grate, little green flames leapt around. Why were they green? Green flames; somehow they were linked in her mind with intense cold. Was it intensely cold tonight? She remembered the saying 'it can be too cold for snow'. But other people said it was never too cold to snow.

She went to the front door and stepped outside for a moment. Yes, it was very cold. Snowing and cold.

Hastily she came back to the fire and resumed her reading. She hopped from poem to poem: ' Christabel'; 'The Ancient Mariner'; ' Goblin Market'; 'The Lotus-Eaters'; 'Hyperion.' She had forgotten her resentment. Time just went on; Yvette didn't look at the clock.

Suddenly, in the middle of 'Michael', she was startled by the phone ringing. She glanced at the clock as she ran to answer it. Midnight.

It was her father. Sorry they were late – they'd rather forgotten about the time. He was calling from The Pheasant – they'd try to drive home now but the roads looked bad. Don't sit up, just go to bed. Oh, and he'd have Clare with him.

Yvette wasn't a bit tired. She went to the landing window and looked out. From here she would be able to watch the Land Rover's lights coming from a great distance up the side valley. She should be able to see them in about half an hour's time. And yes, sure enough, there was a vehicle's lights far down in the valley – her father's, it could be no one else. They came some way then stopped.

It was then that Yvette remembered the binoculars and ran down to the bureau to fetch them. As she trained them on the scene, the Land Rover ceased to be a vague blur. It became two separate lights with two figures moving about, floundering.

Then the vehicle moved a bit more. Another stop. The two figures got out again. This went on for about an hour then the lights finally went out. They must have given up hope and were leaving the Land Rover and walking back.

She shifted the binoculars and looked at the road higher up. It seemed very snowy. She took the binoculars from her eyes but at that very moment of doing so, she had a feeling that something strange and inexplicable had momentarily passed across her field of vision. Something black, moving against the snow. She put the binoculars to her eyes again. Nothing. She laid them down and looked, scanning the scene methodically. No – no – maybe she'd imagined it.

But what was that? She fixed her eyes intently on something black moving very slightly about three hundred yards away. Carefully, she focused the binoculars on the same spot. Yes, there was something there – some strange, black something.

What was it? A sheep? No; all the breeds round here were white. This was all black, or looked so against the snow. What, then? It was on all fours. It moved for a few yards, stopped, floundered then started up again.

Yvette went downstairs and put on her wellies, a thick pullover and a warm coat. She grabbed the spare torch and switched it on. Yes, it was working; the beam flashed brightly across the hallway. She went back to the landing window for a moment to pinpoint the strange object. There it was, just inside the intake fields, close to a wind-blown sycamore.

She went out of the front door. It was cold, very cold. The snow flurried into her eyes. High above, the moon raced through the snow clouds.

Yvette made for the sycamore. The drifts had made the snow patchy. Sometimes she felt the ground right below her feet, hard, icy, frozen. Sometimes there were drifts several feet deep, shaped in exquisite sculptures. She stepped over them and shone her torch beam through the streaming snow towards the sycamore. The black object seemed to have vanished for a moment. Where was it? What was it? It might be something nasty – dangerous. Yet Yvette wasn't in the least frightened, just determined to find out.

She reached the sycamore, looked around, shone her torch beam everywhere. There, over by that slim drift which curved over like a great wave, something was moving. There was a sound, too – a slight, exhausted, panting sound.

Yvette went over and shone the torch down. A shoulder protruded from the foot of the drift. She touched it and the object rolled over. It lay on its back, vaguely moving its limbs like an upturned woodlouse.

She looked at the face. A girl, but not an English girl. The skin was dark. The eyes she couldn't see – the eyelashes seemed to be frozen together.

Yvette tried to speak but the girl didn't understand. Yvette tugged at the girl's shoulders – not heavy but to drag her all the way to the farmhouse would be impossible. But there was that big old wooden sledge, the one her father used to play on with his brothers when they were boys. It was big, strong too. She was sure it was somewhere at the back of the garage.

Yvette moved the dark girl away from the drift to a patch of ground that was almost clear of snow. She tried to convey that she was leaving her for a few moments but it was no use; the girl just clung to Yvette's arm in desperation. Yvette jerked herself free and ran back to the house.

Her father was one of those people who keep everything at the back of the garage, always intending to tidy it up but never did. This was lucky, for in a few moments Yvette had found not only the sledge but also a strong length of rope and an old groundsheet. Thus equipped she returned, pushing her way through the drifts in order to make a rough track for the return journey.

Yvette came back to the dark girl who was still lying on her back and moaning. She folded the groundsheet lengthways and laid it on the sledge, then she lifted the half-frozen girl in her arms and laid her on top. Tying her on with the rope was not easy because the girl rolled and waved her arms in the air. But Yvette wove the rope through the slats of the sledge and secured the two ends with a good reef knot. She took the sledge rope in her hands, and began walking backwards towards the house. The snow had already partially filled the gaps in the drifts. Each one involved a good tug but Yvette was strong and she did it easily.

She came to the front door. Now what? A memory from the distant past swooped through her mind. She remembered as a little girl finding a wounded half-frozen curlew on the moor, bringing it into the house and her mother saying, 'Don't warm it up too abruptly. Put it over there. Let it come to gently.' And so she resisted the impulse to drag the girl right up to the fire and instead she laid her on a rug at the far side of the room.

Her heart jumped as she heard footsteps outside. But of course – it was her father and Clare. She had almost forgotten them. They came in, half stumbling over the sledge which lay across the doorway.

'What on earth is happening?' asked her father, almost gruffly. For him the struggle with the Land Rover had seemed enough adventure for one night.

Yvette waved her hand towards the dark girl on the floor.

'Why – I read something in the paper about an Indian girl who's missing,' murmured her father.

'But it's Kavita!' shouted Clare.

TWENTY-SEVEN

What was happening? Kavita's brain stirred strangely, like an animal wakened in the midst of hibernation. A girl's face appeared, a girl she had never seen before. Auburn hair, freckles. It was as if Kavita had just come into the cinema and this face was flashed on the screen. She closed her eyes, tried to make sense of it, but when she opened them again it was stranger still. The same girl's face was there – but Clare was looking down over her shoulder.

Clare. Of course – that was as it should be. She had been going to Clare. But no, she hadn't found her. She'd lost her way. Vaguely, memories of the last few days seeped back into her consciousness. The wandering in the snow, hopelessly lost, and the feeling of being a fugitive, of being hunted. But by whom? And here she was – somewhere – and there was Clare. But she wasn't at Clare's house. She had never been inside Clare's house, only seen it from a distance yet she was certain this wasn't it. Her last memories were of miles and miles of snowy moorland, no little village, no woods and fields as there were near Clare's.

Kavita looked up at Clare. Clare smiled, bent over her, stroked the hair back from her forehead. Kavita looked round the room and noticed someone else: a man with strong shoulders and a bushy, greying beard. His face was half-familiar – someone she had seen at least once before but she wasn't sure where. All three faces looked down at her and for a moment she felt self-conscious, as if she had to respond in some way to all these questioning looks. She tried to speak but words wouldn't come; only a pained, hissing sound escaped her throat.

'Well,' said the man, 'we'd better phone the police. Tell them to call off the search.'

Kavita felt a spasm of fear. The police – the search – what did that mean? And then she thought of her parents' home. She didn't want to go back. No! She wanted to stay here.

Out of the corner of her eye Kavita saw the log fire burning. The flames leaping warmly up the chimney seemed comforting. She wanted to stay near the warm fire and these kind people forever. And they all looked kind – not just Clare but the man and the auburn-haired girl as well. Kavita wanted to say to them, 'Please, don't send me back.' But no words would come, only the vague hissing sound.

The man left the group and she heard him making a phone call in the next room. Then the auburn-haired girl and Clare took Kavita up to the bathroom, removed her soaking clothes, dried her with a towel and carried her to a bed. She was so exhausted that she was already asleep before they turned out the light.

TWENTY-EIGHT

Kavita's next awakening wasn't sharp and confused like the earlier one but gradual, beautiful. She had a feeling of whiteness about her. Whiteness had become a colour of fear. Those long hours, years seemingly, of wandering in the cold whiteness alone came back to her fleetingly, a stabbing pain. But this whiteness was gentle, comforting. It was the whiteness of the sheets, the pillow cases, the ceiling – and yes, even of the snow.

As she opened her eyes and stirred, she could see the snow piled up against the window pane. But now it was kind, benign, no longer the enemy she had battled with.

She rose up from some deep, deep world of sleep. She felt as if she had been underground for a long time, deep underground, and was now rising up, rising above this strange white world. There were two people, one on either side of her. Those long strands of fair hair – she knew that was Clare without even glancing round. Clare, the eternal fairy godmother who miraculously turned up. And on the other side was Miles, that sad, serious look on his dark features. So sad, so serious; it made her want to laugh.

'My shy boy.' Kavita heard herself speak and realised that her voice had returned. Despite her weakness, she stretched out her hand and drew him down to kiss her.

'I feel so happy now,' Kavita said, 'as if nothing in life could ever be happier. Like passing through some danger – childbirth, perhaps – and then having a great sense of relief.' She was silent for a few moments then she suddenly asked, 'Where am I?'

'You're at Randal's house up on the moors.'

'But how did I get here?'

'Who knows? His daughter Yvette found you in the snow.'

'But why are you here?' Kavita asked, turning to Clare.

'Randal is painting my portrait.' Clare blushed slightly, feeling that this didn't really explain why she had been there in the middle of the night.

'And you?' Kavita asked, turning to Miles.

'Clare told me you were here and I came.'

She lay silent for a bit. An unpleasant thought crossed her mind. 'You're not going to send me back are you? Back to marry that horrid doctor? Not that he's really horrid but I don't want to marry him.' She noticed that Miles was looking puzzled. Of course – he and Clare knew nothing of this.

'Do you want something to eat and drink?' Clare asked, changing the subject.

'Oh yes – yes. I feel quite hungry.'

'Right, we'll get you something.' Clare turned to Miles. 'She can talk when she's eaten.'

Kavita sat up in bed wearing a blue pullover of Clare's, sipping tea and nibbling toast. As she ate her first food for a couple of days she started talking. Her memories rushed at her like a panicking crowd. She told it all; Miles and Clare sat and listened. There was only one point where she bent the truth a fraction: when she came to the original argument with her parents, she didn't use the word 'marriage' in relation to Miles.

Some intuition held her back. She changed it to 'my continuing friendship with Miles'.

Otherwise it all came out: the quarrel, being locked in her bedroom, the escape. It occurred to her as she spoke that she had never consciously decided to escape. It had seemed to be one of those passages in life where events triggered off other events in a sequence beyond her control. Finally, she described walking through the snow, getting lost, sheltering for a while in some lonely sheep fold then carrying on through the snow and the darkness; the closing down of a state of semi-delirium and what little she could remember of being found by Yvette. For a moment she felt as if she were regaling her friends with an adventure story that had no relevance to herself. Then she came to the end.

Silence.

'What happens now?' Clare asked.

'Yes,' replied Kavita. 'That' s the question.'

'Well, you can play at being exhausted for a day or two. That will give us time to think. How do you feel?'

'Embarrassingly well,' Kavita answered, smiling like a child caught in a petty deception. 'I only feel weakness from lack of food.'

'We thought you'd die of pneumonia,' put in Miles.

'Oh, that's the last thing I'd do. "Those whom the gods love die young." The gods probably don't love me.'

'I know what we'll do,' broke in Clare. 'We'll have a conference.'

'A conference about me?'

'Yes. Why not?'

'How will it be then? Shall I lie stretched out on a table, like India about to be partitioned, and you can all gather round and stick little coloured flags in me? "That bit to you and this bit to me. Now this is a demilitarised zone and this we will have a border dispute over." Is that how it's going to be?'

'A bit. It might give us more time, the chance of a compromise so that you're not forced into something you don't want.'

'Maybe. But I hope in the midst of all this that you won't forget that I'm a human being – that I'm a girl.'

'It's all right. Miles won't forget you're a girl,' Clare said, playfully patting Kavita on the cheek.

TWENTY-NINE

The conference as Clare had envisaged it took place but by accident, not by intent. Or perhaps, as Kavita suspected, by a curious alchemy of which Clare alone seemed capable.

It was two days later. The sunlight was brilliant, warm too. Within hours the whiteness of the hills had vanished and great areas of dull russet moorland seemed to heave up from some strange realm below.

Mrs Vora had been on the phone several times, making plans for the family to come and see Kavita – or rather to 'collect Kavita'.

'Oh no, she's not strong enough,' Randal had said, lying somewhat.

'Well, we'll come and see her tomorrow afternoon. Can we get a car up the valley?'

'Yes, I think it's just possible.' Another white lie; it had been possible for several days.

And so that afternoon Dr Vyas drove them over. It was quite a car full. In addition to the doctor there were Mr and Mrs Vora, plus Indu and her three children. Lata, not long out of hospital, clung to her mother. They all trooped into the bedroom where Kavita rested against two pillows, trying to look poorly.

Miles had been with Kavita a few minutes earlier. Now he returned from making some tea to find the Voras settled in, Kavita's mother and father on the far side and Indu sitting on the edge of the bed with Lata in her arms looking unnaturally docile. The two youngest children were playing hide and seek between the dangling folds of the bedcover.

Clare was modelling for Randal when they arrived but immediately, without asking Randal's permission, she got up and went to the bedroom. Neither did she ask the Voras' permission for her intrusion. She sat down in the big chair at the foot of the bed and, by doing so, imposed her personality on the proceedings.

Randal, deprived of his model, merely shrugged his shoulders at the half-finished canvas and decided he might as well join the party.

Kavita glanced round from the bed at this vast gathering. She was torn between a wish to leap out of the window and a fit of giggles. She imposed a numb self-control on herself, suppressing her potential excesses. But how incredibly odd it all was! No one remarked on it; they just gathered round her bed as if it were a normal part of the day's routine. Lying on a table with flags stuck in her would have been scarcely less bizarre.

To begin with there was some desultory conversation about Kavita's state of health. Clare felt impatient. 'Right,' she broke in. 'The big question is Kavita's future.'

'She comes back home when she's fit. That's all there is to it,' said Mrs Vora.

'And what about this story of Kavita being locked in her room because she wouldn't agree to marry Dr Vyas?' Clare persisted.

'Oh,' replied Mrs Vora, 'that was just a joke – a little joke. '

'It didn't seem very funny to me,' Kavita suddenly spat out furiously. 'I could have died in the snow that night.'

'How were we to know you'd do something so stupid?' asked Mrs Vora.

Clare broke in again. 'But what about her agreeing to marry Dr Vyas? How does Kav—'

'It's agreed,' answered Mrs Vora. 'She will marry Dr Vyas when—'

Kavita half-leapt from her pillows. 'Agreed by whom? Not by me. I shall never marry Dr Vyas. He may be a nice man and we're grateful for what he did for Lata. But I don't want to marry him. I want to marry Miles.' She darted a wild glance at Miles. His eyes showed a sort of horrified ecstasy.

'She will do as she's told,' interposed Mrs Vora. 'And that's that.'

'No! Never! Never!' Kavita shrieked out from the bed.

The discussion seemed to have reached a deadlock. Lata stirred in her mother's arms and said, 'Auntie should marry who she wants.'

Indu couldn't stop herself from smiling as she murmured, 'Hush, no one asked you.'

Then Dr Vyas suddenly sat up: 'It may be possible to compromise,' he began. He had once started to train as a lawyer and his lawyer brain was working now; he was almost forgetting that his own happiness was supposed to be at stake.

But Kavita broke in. 'What – cut me in two and each have a half?' She gave Dr Vyas a bitter glance.

Randal stood up. His broad shoulders and imposing appearance forced everyone to look at him. 'Friends, it may seem a bit of a cheek for me to say something since I only came into the story by accident. But still, Kavita is a guest in my house and I'm anxious for her happiness. How about this for an idea? Kavita agrees not to see either of these gentlemen for two years. If, at the end of that time, Miles and Kavita still want to marry they should be allowed to do so. If not, then Kavita bows to her parents' wishes.'

There was silence. Randal's neutrality gave his words added weight. Clare looked at him and smiled then glanced at Kavita. Her look was inscrutable. 'Two years is a long time,' Clare said.

'Six months,' put in Lata.

'Shush,' murmured her mother.

'What about a year?' suggested Dr Vyas.

Kavita and Miles looked at each other. They smiled.

'Yes. We agree,' said Kavita.

Everyone present assented in their own way and the conversation descended to a random exchange of trivialities. Eventually Mr Vora looked at his watch and stood up. 'Ten past four. Aditi's looking after the shop alone. We must go back.'

Soon the car was disappearing down the valley into the early darkness of the February dusk. The peace treaty had been signed.

THIRTY

The need for pretence having ended, Kavita got up and changed into the clean clothes her parents had brought. She and Miles went outside, down the valley to a clump of holly and sycamores. The darkness was almost complete; there was just a vague sense of the receding valley, the last remaining snowdrifts showing white and the street lights far off on the main road.

Kavita took Miles' hands in hers. 'So I suppose this is goodbye – for a year, that is.'

'Yes. Clare will be driving back in about an hour. She can give me a lift.'

'In some ways there's so much to talk about. But I'm tired of talking for once. I just want to feel you close to me. But I must ask you – when I blurted out that I wanted to marry you, what did you feel? I couldn't say anything else because that's what I want. I just want you so much.'

Miles didn't answer, just moved a fraction closer. Kavita flung her arms around him and pressed their bodies close. Miles had never felt Kavita so physically before yet he experienced a strange pain mingled with the pleasure.

'But what did you feel?' Kavita asked again. 'You haven't answered me.'

'Confused.'

'Confused? I'm not surprised. And it's me who's brought you all this confusion.' She laughed abruptly, a sharp little staccato laugh. 'Well,' she persisted, stroking her hands down his back. 'What do you think of me? Say something – just that you like me a tiny bit.'

'Oh Kavita, why ask? Right from the moment I saw you do that snake-charmer dance last summer I was so attracted to you – overwhelmingly – something I'd never felt for a female before.'

'A female, eh? Is that what I am? Not to worry.' She paused for a moment then continued. 'You know, despite everything I feel happier now. A week ago I felt as if I were on a path coming to the head of a valley and all around great rocky cliffs were closing in, too steep to climb. But now I think I see a gap, a little chink, to let me climb up into the daylight. It isn't hopeless, not any more. But why are you sad? I know you're looking sad even though I can't see you. In my mind I can see that sad, shy look. Why is it there?'

'A year is a long time.'

'A year is a tiny little time. Look at that star there, twinkling above the moor. Does it think a year is a long time? No. A year is just a minute turning round, like me pirouetting in a dance.' As she spoke, Kavita released Miles and paced out her dance steps in the darkness.

'There – spring – summer – autumn – winter. Splendid! Back to February – February seventeenth. Remember this date, tattoo it on your memory. It's the day we look forward to. And we must vow to be faithful to each other.'

'Yes, of course.'

Silence for a moment.

'We can write to each other,' Miles said.

'Yes, there is nothing to prohibit that. We just can't meet.'

'We could phone.'

'No – no, I don't like phones. That would be too frustrating. A letter, a long letter, say once a month. But don't send it to my home. Send it to Clare. We'll keep in touch via Clare. I'm sure she'll be agreeable.'

They stopped speaking and held each other close for a long, long time. They could hear no sounds except for the low murmur of each other's breathing. And then, from amongst the holly, a blackbird sang, staccato, rather like Kavita's laugh changed into a minor key. A song of farewell, of sadness – adieu.

END OF PART ONE

PART TWO

ONE

Kavita spent a lot of that year thinking, often in her bedroom with a favourite record playing quietly in the background.

This distance between Miles and herself; what did it mean? It was a distance of time and of space. Time – what was a year? To a small child a year would seem like a lifetime, which is more or less what it is; to an old person, a mere nothing.

She and Miles were somewhere in between. But in a way it was change she feared, rather than time. She knew that the Miles and Kavita who embraced by those holly trees that February evening wouldn't be the same Miles and Kavita who would meet again a year hence.

And now the distance of space was added to that of time. In the late summer Miles went to an art college in York. Kavita left Springwood Sixth-Form College and got a job as a typist. She had passed her A levels with moderate grades, nothing special. She decided she wasn't the academic type; her brains were in her feet as one of the teachers told her. So she got this rather dreary job and devoted her leisure time to dancing. She seemed to reach a peak in this and her services were much in demand. What she wanted for the future was simple: the usual things, marriage, children.

Eventually, when the children grew up, she would become a teacher of dancing, passing on her knowledge to the next generation.

And then she thought of Miles. He was a gifted painter, she knew that; perhaps he was really great, or at least very talented. Either way, she would do her own thing, dancing, and he would do his – or rather they, together, would share their different creativities. Yes, everything seemed clear to Kavita. And the clearer it became, the less the distances of time and space seemed to matter.

*

One day in early autumn, Kavita climbed Tinker's Hill above Holmefield. From here you were supposed to be able to see the towers of York Minster on a clear day.

She couldn't see them but then a stranger pointed them out – there, just to the right of that batch of cooling towers. Kavita looked intently at those two tiny strokes of white set against the distant blue.

Thereafter she liked to think of Miles in this way: distant, yet very definitely there. And when the time seemed to be dragging, she thought of Rama and Sita and their long years of exile in the forest. But they had eventually come back together and returned to their kingdom. Yes, she and Miles would return to their kingdom too, soon, quite soon.

TWO

A year: how do we portray a year in a drama during which the hero and heroine do not meet? Should we just bring down the curtain and proclaim an interval? No. We will bridge the gap with four short scenes.

SPRING

The line of daffodils leading up to Tostenland Church is in bloom. The morning is clear, with the grey mist down in the Fielden Valley fading quickly. Pigeons fly in the warming light. The bank sides are filling up with bluebells.

Within the church they are singing the final hymn: 'O Love of Whom Is Truth and Light.' The sunlight streams through the 'Lord Is My Shepherd' window. A tiny tint of red from the shepherd's robe falls on the bride's dress. Clare glances down, smiles.

The hymn ends and the organist begins the postlude. Yvette picks up the train of Clare's dress. Down the chancel steps, turn left through the porch and out into the brilliant sunshine.

The flock of friends and well-wishers – half the village, in fact – follow on behind. Photos. The vicar beams benignly as the April sunlight plays on his rosy cheeks. His wife smoothes back her greying hair then reaches for her camera. Miles goes and sits on a gravestone, a bit apart. He looks across at Clare as if deciding on a portrait, studying every fold of her snow-white dress.

Photos over, they walk down the path to the car. But the children have tied the churchyard gates together. It's a custom – they've done this for hundreds of years in Tostenland. The children won't untie them until the bridegroom has thrown some money. Randal smiles, fumbles in his pocket. He's forgotten about this. Panic. What to do?

But Clare has not forgotten. She's slyly concealed a bag of money in the wires holding her bouquet. She tugs it out and slips it discreetly to Randal behind the folds of her wedding dress. He smiles even more, throws the money towards the children.

The gates are untied.

SUMMER

Summer, late summer to be precise, when the days already tremble on the edge of autumn. The Ouse – the Yorkshire Ouse, about a mile from York. The time – mid-afternoon. By the river banks, a group of art students are gathered, five of them, their easels set up and boxes of oils, acrylics and watercolours laid out according to taste.

What will Phil make of this landscape? He despises twee, pretty-pretty little pictures; He comes from Barnsley, concentrates on miners, slag heaps and outside privies. But how can he avoid a pretty-pretty little picture here?

Beyond, on the far bank, an ash tree dips its low sweeping branches into the slowly rippling river. Meadows stretch out wide and flat; Friesians graze or doze in the shade. One cow has waded into the stream and is drinking, the great Victorian cliché come to life. And in the distance is York – churches, walls, Minster all white in the wilting heat. Yes, those two western towers of the Minster are the focus of everything; the river, the meadows, the ash tree boughs – they all point towards them.

'Phil's found inspiration,' shouts Serena. 'He's just spotted an outside privy three miles off. The old artistic juices are flowing. I can see it all.'

Miles glances across at her. In a way she seems familiar – that full figure, fluffy lightish-brown hair. Looks incredibly young to be wearing a wedding ring.

She leans towards Phil's canvas. 'But he's painting a tree! A tree! Good God – trees went out in the last century. Constable said all there was to say about trees. After Constable there can be no more trees. Hasn't anyone told you? What on earth d'you think your canvas can say about that ash tree which hasn't been said a million times before?'

'I shall say that it's an ash tree and the light dappled by the shadows of the foliage is beautiful. OK – for once I'll be seduced. Perhaps this is really my metier – maybe at the end of this I'll forget slag heaps and outside privies. Might get a job illustrating Patience Strong.'

Patience Strong! Miles thought of his mother in times of crisis, sitting in the living room clutching Patience Strong's *Quiet Corner.* That curious world of religious sentimentality he had been brought up in – somehow he recoiled from it, like an overdose of golden syrup.

But there were so many worlds! The world Kavita had ushered him into, that world of Hinduism, dance, music, rich colours and smells and tastes. A stranger, more beautiful world than he had ever known – ever would know.

Yet how unconnected were those worlds. Not in the way that a symphonic movement modulates from one key to another. No. More abrupt – far more abrupt. More like a television; one channel is showing and then someone presses a button and without warning one is plunged into something totally different.

And now it had happened again. Wham! The plain of York – flat, bicycles everywhere, poplars, big wide skies – and the eternal vista of York Minster. Why were there so many worlds?

Each one was a lifetime's study. And yet in a way every human being was their own little world. Ken, for example, the young American who was lashing on acrylics beside him. What did he see in that restful riverside scene? God knows, for somehow his brain transformed it into lines, squares and diagonals that he painted with evangelical fervour. And Katie down by the river – what did she see? She alone hadn't brought an easel, merely a small sketch pad, a pencil (yes, just one), a rubber and a pencil sharpener. Thus equipped, she was drawing a single sprig of elder leaves that overhung the water. She had rejected the river itself – the ash tree, the cows, the distant cathedral. Only that sprig, that sprig of elder leaves. But it was valid, it was a good drawing.

Miles, for his part, was content to be a camera. He hadn't come to terms with this world sufficiently to be anything else. For a moment he wondered how Chagall would have seen it. Perhaps the towers of the Minster would have been important low down in the picture, with the river lower still. And then up in the sky he and his sweetheart (wife?) floating serenely, she clutching a bouquet of flowers. A donkey braying incongruously in a corner of the sky – a fiddler likewise – and a giant fish paddling its way through the lower canvas. For a moment he pictured Kavita floating in the sky above York Minster. But no, she would only fall; his imagination couldn't construct a scaffolding to hold her.

And so, he would be a camera. He would even paint in that cow drinking from the river. Maybe Constable *had* said it all, for all time. But it seemed a tale worth repeating.

AUTUMN

Yvette was gathering blackberries on top of a small hillock partway down the valley. She liked the blackberries themselves and the excuse for being out of doors, getting something free. And finally the cooking – jams, jellies, all so delicious.

But Yvette wasn't quite so happy this year. It was Clare. Clare was lovely, of course, not the notorious evil stepmother of the fairy tale – nothing like that. But this time last year Yvette had been the woman of the house for all that she was only fifteen. She had started to cook, made meals for her father, was getting better and better. But now Clare was installed; she was the woman of the house, imposing a quiet authority in numerous minor ways.

Before her father's marriage, Yvette had loved Clare. But now...? Well, she still loved her. Clare was so kind, so lovely in every way. But now she was close up and no longer the idolised figure, there were lots of trivial annoyances.

That afternoon Yvette had wanted to do some cooking – coconut cakes. She had walked towards the kitchen, her cookery books in her hand. But Clare was already there and the cooking utensils Yvette wanted were in use. Yvette knew that she only had to go in, ask if she could use a corner of the table and wash up the various items when Clare no longer needed them. But she would have to ask – not like the old days when she just walked in. And so Yvette pretended she wasn't walking towards the kitchen. No, the living room instead.

She stood for a moment looking out at the sunshine. Yes, she would go and pick blackberries. And in a way it was far nicer to be outside on top of that hillock, the warm afternoon sun beating on the valley side, on the bracken now turned to russet.

Yvette soon forgot about Clare. She turned to musing, thinking about her boyfriend Simon. She was fond of him but there were problems. She would have liked to talk to an older woman. A year ago, Clare would have been the obvious person – Clare, the semi -mother, semi-eider sister. But Clare was too close now.

Her thinking lapsed and she concentrated on the blackberries. She had brought an enamel can with a wire handle. Rather a big can, a bit optimistic perhaps. But this was a good patch and not many people knew about it. She picked away, all other things in life seeming distant compared with her wish to fill the container. But how could they eat all the berries if she filled it? Oh well – turn them into jelly.

It was almost dusk before the can was full. Yvette clasped the handle and staggered back up the valley, changing hands as the wire cut into her fingers. She emerged from the lower valley with its brambles and scattered trees. Beyond were a few fields, their house and the moorland. The very last tree was a sycamore – *the* sycamore – the one beside which she had found Kavita that strange night back in January. A strange night – rather terrible in fact – yet exciting, beautiful.

She thought of that first sight of Kavita, a weird dark animal crawling in the snow. From that weird creature had appeared this pretty Indian girl, like a fine butterfly emerging from an ugly pupa. Strange. But yes – Kavita: that was the person to confide in. Think of what Kavita had gone through, locked in her room because she refused to marry a man she didn't love. That was romantic. That was great. Yes, Kavita had really seen life.

Calmed by this thought, Yvette carried the big can across the last stretch to the door. Clare came out of the kitchen, her long fair hair covered with a scarf. She was so pleased to see her – and the blackberries – that Yvette regretted any unkind thing she had ever thought about her. But then – oh well, never mind.

WINTER

January: the night cold, the moon rising frostily, dull orange, slipping up the sky between furrows of cloud. The ground skiffed with snow, frozen, sparkling in the street lamps. The odd snowflake, large and slow, falling wearily down past the high buildings.

Amongst these high buildings one window is brilliantly lit – the art gallery. Cars drive up outside. Women wrap their fur coats closer as they cross the few yards from the car to the main doors. Saris spread momentarily on the iced snow - to be lifted quickly by a dark, ungloved hand. This is the opening night of the Indian art exhibition. The mayor is to attend (that big car over there? – no – no, the mayor's car is even bigger).

In the foyer the long table is spread with tablecloths and three girls behind it are serving wine: white, red and rosé. The mayor is to make the opening speech; nothing much can happen until he arrives.

Kavita and Indu stepped towards the table.

'Wine – red, white, rosé?'

'No – no – I don't drink.'

'Oh, you'll be the Indian dancer,' said one of the wine girls, looking at Kavita's parrot-green sari.

'Yes. Can you point me to the person in charge?'

'Yes, over there. Mr Twisleton, Secretary of the local Arts Council.'

Kavita remembered him from the National Arts Day celebration – her snake-charmer dance, the first meeting with Miles. That seemed a long time ago. But there he was with his bushy black beard, running around in a tizz trying to organise everything, exactly as she remembered him.

'Ah Miss Vora and...?' He turned to Indu who was more plainly dressed in pink. 'I thought we only had one dancer.'

'That's right,' answered Indu. 'I'm just her sister.'

'My sister and my second teacher,' put in Kavita.

'Yes, it was a case of the pupil excelling the teacher,' said Indu modestly but correctly.

'I wish the mayor would hurry up,' muttered Mr Twisleton distractedly. 'He's always late. Sometimes he doesn't come at all.' Then in Kavita's ear: 'He's an awful speaker in any case.'

'Perhaps,' she replied, 'it would be better if I made the speech and the mayor did the dance.'

'Oh no – we don't want comedy turning into farce! Ah – but there he is.'

'His Worshipful the Mayor.' The mace-bearer's voice boomed out. The mayor advanced. He had a face rather like a child's portrayal of the sun, with eyes and mouth beaming diffused benevolence. His mayoral chain reflected back the foyer lights as it bounced on his broad chest. He advanced to a low rostrum wondering what the hell to say. He knew nothing about Indian art – nothing about art, in fact.

He glanced around hastily. Bright colours. Good. The mayor liked bright colours. So did the mayoress; her dress was scarlet and her stockings were purple. And so the mayor cobbled together his speech as he went along. With a generous sprinkling of 'ums' and 'ahs', he managed to string together an impressive collection of nothing-in-particulars for the space of about five minutes.

Rapturous applause.

Mr Twisleton stepped forward with a swing of his bushy beard. 'And now Miss Kavita Vora will do a sequence of Indian dances. I have watched Miss Vora dancing on several occasions and I am sure we are all going to have a treat this evening. Oh, and ladies and gentlemen – if you could remember that these are religious dances and abstain from smoking or drinking whilst Miss Vora is dancing.'

Kavita stepped forward and made the namaste greeting, hands together, slight bow, then she did three dances, explaining each one beforehand. Kavita felt well – fit, lively. Miles would be coming back to her soon – only a month – and she danced as if Miles were actually in the audience, standing there in the foyer admiring her.

In the short gaps between the dances she glanced at Indu and Indu made her characteristic gesture: a single finger held in the air. Kavita knew the sign. It meant: 'Bravo – you're doing well.'

And then, just as the last dance was ending, Kavita felt her spontaneous exuberance ebbing. She did everything correctly but something alien had struck her. A pair of eyes in the audience focused on her, which she did not like. As the applause burst forth, she looked at those eyes. Yes – Dr Vyas.

He had probably not meant to break his side of the agreement, would have been invited by the organisers as a prominent member of the Indian community. Most likely he didn't even know that Kavita was dancing. But still – looking across at him standing there at the very back, she felt a chill. He made her think of a vulture on its perch waiting to come down and peck at a corpse. Kavita shuddered. Even as she took her bows and outwardly smiled she shuddered.

'Well,' asked Indu, 'shall we go round and meet people, socialise, look at the pictures?'

'No. I feel tired – not quite myself. Let's go home.'

‘Oh well,’ replied Indu disappointedly, turning to the door.

*

And thus a year passed by.

THREE

It was February the seventeenth. The long year during which they had agreed not to meet was over. Back in the late autumn when she had bought her next year's diary, the first thing Kavita had done was to draw a large asterisk in red biro across that date. Each day she had turned over a page as she entered up the small nothingnesses of her life. Now at last she had reached to where that great sunset – no, sun*rise* – loomed red above the page.

Underneath the asterisk she had written '6 p.m.' in blue. This was the time, as she remembered it, when Miles had finally released her from his arms and got into Clare's car. Yes, she must be precise. Six p.m. After that she could see Miles openly. Everything had worked out right; she had been true to him and he to her. There was nothing to worry about.

She returned from the office. Dusk fell. She welcomed the fading light, the darkness, the odd star piercing the murky sky. Six p.m. Something would happen. Perhaps Miles would walk in, just like that. But this seemed unlikely. It was Wednesday; he wouldn't be home from York till the weekend. Kavita had half-expected a letter that morning but no luck. A phone call, that was more likely.

Indu and her three children turned up at five. The children wanted to see a programme on television. They moved the volume knob to very loud but not loud enough to drown the shrieks of excitement from the two youngest. Kavita went into the kitchen and helped her mother prepare the meal.

Six fifteen. The phone rang. Kavita rushed to it. 'Have you got the other sort of tomato sauce in yet? Can't stand the old stuff and I'm not walking three hundred yards for rubbish.'

It was old Mrs Sykes from two streets away. Kavita almost cursed aloud as she ran into the shop and verified that the new sort was indeed available.

Another phone call of a similar nature five minutes later convinced Kavita that Miles had forgotten all about the date. Then, just as the children's shouts were reaching a crescendo, the phone rang again.

'It's Miles here – can I speak to Kavita?'

'It *is* Kavita, you silly— Oh, damn those children! One moment. Shut up! Shut up! For once in your little lives be quiet.'

Malti and Kishore weren't used to their favourite auntie getting cross. They were suddenly silent.

The rest of the conversation consisted of instructions about the train – what time it arrived, what to do if it was late. How aggravating. There was so much Kavita wanted to say, so many parts of her mind she wanted to pour down that little cable to Miles. But no, it was no use. This was always the way with the romantic climaxes of life: they always, always, scattered into trivialities. But what did it matter? By Friday they would be together. So much they could talk about then.

They were meeting in Holmefield then taking a bus to The Pheasant right on the edge of the moors. They would live it up like Randal and Clare sometimes did. It was more than they could afford but this was something special.

'Right, you can make as much noise as you like now,' Kavita shouted to the children as she laid down the receiver.

FOUR

It was those tropical fish in the corner of the restaurant. They were dancing – that was how it seemed to Kavita – dancing in tune with her own happiness. She was sitting there in her beautiful cerise sari – how soft it felt against her hands – and Miles was opposite, so loving and attentive. The food was exquisite – that garlic bread and the small glass of ruby wine – and beyond the window the slow afterglow of sunset shown in rippled reflections in a vast moorland reservoir.

She was so happy. Nothing in life could ever be more perfect. Never! And those angelfish, they seemed to know; they seemed to be dancing somewhere in the caverns of her own mind.

Miles, too, seemed to see things from a new viewpoint. It was as if he had almost forgotten how physically beautiful Kavita was. The girl he remembered from a year ago was ethereal, spiritual. That last memory of her, the receding figure as Clare had driven him away in the car, had been like a spirit, a waif, not a physical girl at all. But now, as if for the first time, he noticed that Kavita was terribly pretty.

They ate avidly but what they did mostly was talk. Kavita pestered Miles with questions about his life at York. What had he done? Who had he met? What pictures had he painted? For herself, there seemed little to tell: the studies for A level; the exams; her rather boring job as a typist. But she dug up from her memory all the small details that might amuse him.

And thus the evening wore on. The meal was good (chicken crepes for Miles, a special vegetarian meal for Kavita); the waiters polite; the fire burned brightly; the fish swam merrily.

And yet... And yet... When they were going back on the bus, Kavita felt a strange sense of disappointment. Why? She couldn't explain it. She fought against it. Yet when she was back in her room, this sense of disappointment was her predominant emotion. Why? Why? But all she knew was that in some irrational way she was unhappy.

FIVE

The weekends passed; the strange sense of disappointment continued. What was it? There was nothing; everything was all right. They talked of the future – marriage, plans for many things. But there was something wrong, something Kavita couldn't define.

She confided in Clare. 'Do you think,' Clare asked, 'that Miles has something on his mind? Something he won't tell you about but which you can somehow sense?'

'Maybe.'

'Why not ask him straight out? Bring your secret unhappiness into the open.'

*

The next time Kavita and Miles saw each other, they went for a walk on the edge of the golf course. As they came home, watching the dusk gather in the valley, Kavita did exactly as Clare had suggested. She rather hoped that Miles would just say, 'Oh heavens – you're imagining things,' and that would be that. But he didn't. He stopped, turned pale, put his hand to his forehead.

Kavita felt a chill running through her. 'Oh my God. Is there really something you're keeping back from me?'

'Well…'

'No, please – don't tell me now.' She put her finger up to his mouth as if pushing the words back down his throat. 'I couldn't bear any upset at the moment. Next time perhaps but not now.'

And so they continued walking back to Wesley Street in silence.

SIX

Miles thought about what he would say to Kavita when next they met. It was that year, that year when nothing much had happened. But how could a whole year pass and nothing much happen? Impossible when one is young.

Yes, it was Serena. That was basically what he had to tell her about – Serena. He had thought to tell her that very first evening at The Pheasant but everything had seemed so perfect – the food, the view, and above all Kavita herself. Even the fish in the aquarium seemed to be saying to him: 'Don't talk too much. Just leave things as they are. There will be time later.' But the later times had been just as impossible. And now somehow Kavita had got wind of it. How exasperating females were, the way they sniffed out problems like truffle hounds. Anyway, there it was. He would have to tell her – next time.

Serena. Miles thought back to their first meeting – well, not really the first but what he thought of as their first meeting – by the river bank. Not that he had noticed her especially. There were so many impressions to take in during those early weeks in York. The town itself, its intricate filigree of ancient towers; its stubbled growth of timbered buildings; the flat wakeful river and the wide clean fields. And then the other students. The lectures. The course. The new ideas and techniques. So much to take in. And Serena was only a fragment of it all.

What he had gathered was that she had a soft sort of kittenish beauty, was a few years older than him, had brown fluffy hair and wore a wedding ring. He learnt that, unlike most of the students, she actually lived in York in an old house just within the walls and her husband was a young businessman. Before college she had worked – what was it? – something in the artistic line. Anyway, she was just a tiny fragment of an impression.

Miles didn't want to be overwhelmed by York. His life, his real life, lay on the other side of Yorkshire. He saw it all as if summed up in a single picture: a beautiful Indian girl in a cerise sari and beyond the dark stone terraced houses, the mills, the grey of the distant moorland. That was the picture he belonged to, not York. He felt towards York like a woman going into the village shop for a pound of butter and determined not to be side-tracked by anything else. All Miles wanted from York was his art qualification, nothing more. Once he had that, he would be away.

But York was a place you couldn't really ignore and neither could he ignore Serena. She seemed to take a serious interest in him and in lots of subtle ways thrust herself on his attention. He was a little flattered by the notice of this attractive woman. She asked him about his work; they looked through each other's folios. Then she questioned him about his background and found out about Kavita. In a way Miles felt reluctant to talk about Kavita – it cheapened her somehow. And yet in another way it was nice to be able to talk about her; it brought her image closer. Serena seemed very interested yet she didn't reciprocate by saying much about herself.

Miles had met her husband only once. He was a man of scrupulous politeness with whom Miles felt nothing in common.

Once, a propos of nothing that had gone before, Serena suddenly said, 'You are an innocent boy.' It reminded him of the way Kavita called him 'my shy boy' – but with a twist.

Yes, Serena seemed determined that he should notice her. One day she mentioned some variety show in town that she wanted to go to. A few days later, as they were waiting for a lecture, she thrust a small piece of purple paper into his hand. Miles looked at it blankly. 'Your ticket for the variety show, you silly,' she whispered in his ear. Afterwards they made arrangements: they would meet at the end of Petergate, facing across to the Minster, at six p.m.

By ten to six Miles was already there. It was dusk, October dusk filled with starlings and fallen leaves. The clock on the Minster struck. It had a note of doom, as if striking the hour when a murderer was to be hanged. There was no sign of Serena; maybe she wouldn't come. But no, there she was turning the corner. She kissed him, took him by the arm and led him to a noisy cafe. Miles looked at her across the table; she seemed more sophisticated this evening, had put on more makeup than usual although nothing excessive.

The show started with the usual chorus of dancing girls, their smiles clinging like limpets to their ruby lips, their scarlet dresses flung back as they tossed their legs into the footlight-flooded air.

'Isn't this jolly?' murmured Serena.

He wasn't sure if this was sarcasm. Certainly it was jolly, terribly jolly – there was no doubt about that. The dancing girls, the ribald jokes, the comedian's stock gags about Aberdonians and Irishmen. Jolly! And Miles was excited – troubled as well: troubled, excited, confused. Not by the show, no – although somehow that was part of it as well. The girls in the chorus flung tinsel from their smile-set eyes whilst vaguely he felt Serena's thigh pressed against his somewhere in the darkness.

The show was over. 'You'll come round to my house for a coffee,' Serena said.

'Yes – yes.' *She wants to introduce me properly to her husband,* Miles thought, *to bring me into her circle of friends.*

The house appeared quite posh, old, timbered. Serena unlocked the door, and took him through to the kitchen. 'My husband's out with his girlfriend. He won't be home tonight.' She smiled.

Miles felt his heart kick like a chorus girl's leg.

Serena carried on making the coffee. 'You take milk – sugar?'

'Oh yes,' Miles said absent-mindedly.

'Two?'

'No, just one.'

She poured out the cups, plopped in the milk and sugar and placed them on a small tray. Miles moved in front of her, uncertain which door to open.

'In there.'

He pushed open a door, switched on the light and a beautiful small drawing room appeared: pink upholstery, china ornaments, brassware.

Serena turned on the electric fire. They sat together on the sofa, drinking the coffee. Nothing much was said.

They laid the empty cups back on the tray. *What now?* Miles wondered. At that moment he was still in control. He remembered his vow to Kavita; it was there repeating itself, a distant throb somewhere in his brain. And something else flashed vividly in his mind: a memory, a distant memory – distant but powerful.

And then it was he who made the first move, Miles not Serena. He stretched out his hand and touched the back of her neck, moved his fingers over her collar and across the upper part of her breasts. She fell forward, pressed him into the corner of the sofa, quickly kissed his face, her hair falling carelessly on to his forehead and into his eyes.

The next ten minutes were something of a blur. The whispered, 'Let's go upstairs'; climbing the wooden staircase – the top step creaked; the bedroom, slightly chill; undressing, Serena throwing her garments one by one on the floor.

For a moment she stood before him, not touching. Then, with a tiny blow on his shoulder – gentle but deft – she pushed him back on the bed, laughing at his surprise. She fondled and kissed his whole body. He was hers now, completely. A thousand vows signed in blood would have been null and void against this power of sensuality.

When it was over and they lay in the glow of their bodies, Serena stretched her bare arm across the pillow and tugged at a curtain. Miles lifted his face from the cooling sweat on her breasts and looked out to the floodlit front of the Minster. Was it really the same building he had stood beside at six o'clock, only a few hours ago? Everything was changed. For a moment he thought of Kavita then he lowered his head and kissed Serena's lips for what seemed like the thousandth time.

After a while she spoke. 'You'll enjoy it even more the next time. You'll be more relaxed.'

The next time? Miles hadn't thought that far ahead. The present seemed too overwhelming.

'We've met before,' Miles said. 'I suddenly realised as we sat on that sofa – something about seeing your hair against the edge of your shoulder.'

'I know. I knew it all along. That quiet intense little boy who once came to the life-drawing class and never returned. I often wondered what became of him – and now I know. He's here, right here.' And she ran her hands down his back and over his hips and drew him close to her one last time.

*

They remained lovers through the winter. Whenever convenient, when her husband was away, Serena asked him round to that old timbered house. He was happy. He couldn't resist the soft femininity that she offered. And the strangest thing was that to him it was all somehow linked with Kavita. It was as if this part of his life were somehow an introduction, a prelude. *With Kavita it will be even more beautiful*, he thought.

February drew close and He told Serena it couldn't go on. February the seventeenth: the end of the separation.

'That's all right. I knew this was coming. It was good while it lasted.'

*

Now this was all in the past, a very distant past so it seemed. He still saw Serena and she smiled as they passed in the corridor. Sometimes his wanderings took him along the street with the old timbered house and he glanced at the upstairs windows. How long ago it seemed but it was only a few weeks.

So whatever had happened, it was in the past. The present was Kavita and the present problem was how to tell Kavita. How would she react? Would she understand? Would she realise that he had thought of her all the time? That this closeness with Serena had really been part of his relationship with Kavita? Would she accept that, realise it was true, understand how he had felt inside. Miles wasn't sure and he was frightened. But perhaps if he were completely open, just told her exactly how he had felt – did feel – she would accept. But... No – no buts. He braced himself.

SEVEN

Kavita was tense all that week. She wanted the weekend to come quickly so she could get over this revelation, whatever it might be. Sometimes she tried to puzzle out what it was but no; her mind went into a sort of grey blur whenever she forced it in that direction.

And so she met him off the train on Saturday afternoon with a feeling of dread. How different from that first weekend after the separation. She thought he looked pale and tired. They kissed; she took his hand and they went along the street to a cheap Italian cafe for a cup of tea.

The place was busy but everyone else seemed to be absorbed. The fat, middle-aged proprietor was taking orders and shouting instructions; some Caribbean youths played noisily on a fruit machine; a few pensioners tucked in greedily to late lunches.

Kavita thought this would be a good place to talk. She leant across the table. 'OK – tell me what's on your mind.'

Miles started to tell her about Serena, quietly, nervously. He didn't look in her eyes but fixed his gaze on the whirling surface of the tea as he stirred the cup a hundred times more than was necessary. He had decided to tell her everything. He went into detail.

Kavita felt a gathering anger as the story progressed. At the point where he and Serena were going up to the bedroom her fury reached flashpoint. Suddenly she leapt up, grabbed Miles by the lapels of his jacket and pulled him towards her.

'D'you know, I could kill you right now!' she screamed. 'Kill you! If I had a knife, I'd stab it right there in that weak little heart of yours.' She jabbed at his ribs with her hand so violently that Miles gasped. 'D'you know what I went through for you? That night in the snow, only one thing kept me going – that I loved you. I don't need other men to tell me I'm beautiful though plenty do. I know I am – and all that beauty was for you. I was saving it, saving every jot of myself for you. And what happens? The very first woman who tempts you? You go to bed with her!'

As she spoke, Kavita let go of Miles and made a wild gesture with her hands. One backward sweep sent her cup and saucer flying across the cafe floor. Everyone stopped and looked at them. The proprietor ran forward.

'Madam! Madam, I will have to send for the police. This is second time today. This morning a dispute about a cheeseburger. This fellow says—'

'Let's go,' Kavita muttered. She led Miles, actually took his hand like a trembling child's, and walked straight through the broken crockery and out of the door.

She dropped his hand and for an hour or two they wandered aimlessly around the town in sullen silence. Then Miles got his bus back to the village. They parted without a kiss, with scarcely a goodbye.

EIGHT

They met a few times after that, just a few, but the zest had gone out of their relationship and Kavita's spontaneous affection seemed to have been replaced by a slow murmur of resentment. Miles had never seen this side of her, never guessed that it might be there. When he looked in her eyes that soft loving look had gone. In her pupils there seemed to lurk something else, like a dark snake coming out of a cave, ready to strike.

Where were they going? What were they doing? They seemed to be on a road that led nowhere, a cul-de-sac. And what could they do? What could remove this wall of hostility that blocked the way in front of them? Nothing? Or time? Nothing, it seemed.

A few weeks later, Miles received a letter from Kavita. He looked down at it as it lay on the doormat of his flat in York, saw the familiar writing, the familiar postmark. Only a short while ago it would have been so welcome. But then – perhaps she was writing to say that she forgave him, that the quarrel was over.

The cold opening words soon mangled that hope.

Dear Miles,

I have been thinking so much recently about this thing that has happened between us. I can't get rid of the hatred I now feel for you. Yes, hatred – no milder word would be true. Let us not meet for a while. It is bringing us no pleasure. I am not saying goodbye forever, just for a while.

If, when I have thought things through, I still feel that I want you I will let you know. But please don't pester me. Don't even write.

If this letter hurts you, remember it is only written because you have hurt me so terribly.

Kavita

NINE

Miles crumpled the letter into his pocket and walked out in the direction of the art college, half hoping that a car would knock him down as he crossed the busy road. In the entrance corridor he passed Serena of all people. He knew she was going to smile at him but he suddenly felt intensely angry and embarrassed. He noticed the smile kill itself on her lips as their eyes met. Not so long ago, Serena's smile would have seemed like a bonus – a tiny stream falling into his ocean of happiness. But not now: he felt he hated her.

*

Serena soon realised that something was wrong. The smiles ceased as they passed; they scarcely spoke to each other. In fact, everything virtually stopped for Miles. His art work went to nothing; the pens, pencils and brushes just wouldn't respond as if they too were joined against him. He longed to talk to someone about how he felt, but who?

His mother now seemed to be locked in a world of sentimental Christianity that Miles no longer wanted to enter. Once they had been close, but not now. He had never been close to his stepfather, although Miles knew that his stepfather had rather taken to the lovely Indian girl. And in a way there was a strange unspoken bond between them now, something there had never been before. But the moment things were put into words and his parents asked questions about what was happening, Miles was filled with an intense annoyance mingled with pain. His mother was like Kavita in that she could at once sniff out something wrong.

Who else was there?

The only person he knew well in York was Serena but the idea of confiding in her sickened him, although he knew that she would have been kind and perhaps even genuinely distressed at what had happened. No one else. His mind was a blank.

*

One evening, when this depression was at its blackest, he happened to be walking past the art gallery. It was spring, the daylight hours drawn out to cover these hours in a wide skirt of sunshine. Everything seemed to mock his despair: the starlings chattering in the pseudo-classical cliff face of the dark stone gallery; the crocuses drifting their saffron robes over the April earth.

Yet one thing did awaken his interest: a poster, *Retrospective Exhibition of the work of Randal Bramley*. Randal. Miles thought of that strong confident figure he had always admired. He remembered that day last spring, the wedding at Tostenland, the tied gates, the money thrown to the children. And Clare – Clare. Why had he thought there was no one he could talk to?

Miles looked more closely at the poster: '*Exhibition open to the public April 30th until June 10th.*' April 30th – that was tomorrow, which meant that presumably the opening was tonight. And yes, sure enough, various people were going in through a side door. With one of those sudden decisions of which his normally faltering character seemed capable, Miles decided to go in. Of course he should have had an official invitation but he knew that no one was ever so petty minded as to actually check on invitations.

At the door an auburn-haired freckle-faced girl handed him a catalogue. Yvette. She looked so grown-up. She smiled, a knowing smile.

Miles took his glass of red wine from the table and started to look round the pictures. He ignored the portraits. The landscapes, watercolours mostly, were slapped on with Randal's usual panache. The subjects were valleys, mills, cottages, hills, the whole of the West Riding. Miles felt he loved it again. The last few weekends at home had been wretched but now, seen through Randal's eyes, something came back to life in him – an old love.

As he stood in front of a picture of Hardcastle Crags, Miles felt a hand on his arm and turned to find Randal's broad shoulders looming above him. 'Lovely to see you, young man. But I could have sworn I hadn't— Never mind. How are you doing? What you painting these days?'

The conversation stayed on art for some while. Eventually Miles asked, 'Is Clare here?'

'No – no, she's a little unwell. Nothing much, a little Bramley on the way, you know. But come across and see us all sometime – say next weekend.'

For Miles, that next weekend had abruptly taken on an interest.

TEN

Miles was pleased that Clare was alone when he called. Not that he didn't like Randal – far from it – but right now he wanted to be alone with Clare. So he learnt with a sense of relief that Randal was out somewhere painting and Yvette was in town.

And Clare looked so lovely as she opened the door. The indisposition Randal had referred to must have been mild, for Miles' main impression was of that strange look of deep well-being that women sometimes assume during pregnancy. For a moment the thought went through Miles' mind: what if things had worked out differently, if he had come together with Clare instead of Kavita?

He looked at her. 'Can I kiss you?' he asked quite shyly. Miles had never kissed Clare except on her wedding day.

'Of course.'

He went to kiss on the cheek as she moved to kiss him on the lips and they met in confusion at the edges of their mouths. She laughed at the mistake and led him into the living room. A log fire was burning for, despite being spring, it was still cold. Beyond the windows he could see the snowdrifts lingering in the cloughs of the higher hills.

He sat down on some cushions. Clare brought in the tea. As soon as the polite formalities were over Miles told her his troubles, hiding nothing.

'Well, what can I do now?' he asked.

'Let me think.'

Clare got up and stood for quite some while looking out of the window in silence. Miles stayed by the fire looking at her fair hair lying carelessly across the folds of her green dress, hearing a lark singing high up above the moorland.

Eventually she turned, came back to the fire and took his hand. 'I know she forbids it but my advice is that you write Kavita one short letter – just one – perhaps only a few sentences. But make it absolutely clear that she's the person in your life who really matters, that you still love her, that if she can find it in her heart to forgive you, you'll be waiting for her. ' She looked at Miles for an answer.

'Yes. Yes, I'll do exactly that.'

Clare couldn't stop a smile spreading over her lips. It always amused her that Miles viewed her as the Greeks looked on the Delphic oracle.

Miles looked at her again; he couldn't stop looking at her. He felt an intense wish to hold her in his arms. He leant forward.

She seemed to guess what he wanted. 'You can put your arms around me if you want,' she said.

Miles did so, laying his head on her shoulder. They lay thus for some while. For Miles the predominant feeling was not of aroused emotions but of a wonderful comfort that seemed to flow from Clare's body.

Eventually Clare said, 'There's Randal coming down the hillside with his easel under his arm.'

She didn't make a move but Miles thought it wouldn't be quite the thing for Randal to find him with his arms around Clare. He released her; they kissed briefly and then went to the door to greet Randal.

ELEVEN

A few days later Kavita received Miles' letter. She was angry when she saw it. All the hatred and fury that she had felt during the row in the cafe welled up again. She thought of tearing it up unread. But no – she read it. Again she thought of destroying it but instead she folded the single sheet in four and placed it under a dupatta in a drawer.

TWELVE

The summer came and went. It was a good summer, so people said: long days, hot sun, clear skies. But for Kavita it all seemed darker than the deepest winter. She longed for something – for many things but above all for release from that numbing hatred. But all that she saw was the hot sun beating on the dry, dusty pavements and seeming to echo back the aridity of her own emotions.

Autumn came. It was a time for celebrations. On September 7th there would be the annual festival for the birth of Krishna, which Kavita loved almost as much as Dwali. And then, only a week later, there was her parents' ruby wedding anniversary. There was to be a big party for all the Vora family plus their relations and friends.

Kavita wondered how on earth the living room was going to hold them all. During the evening various people would be asked to provide entertainment. All the Vora children had some sort of talent, especially Aditi who sang and Kamlesh who played the sitar. And of course Kavita would dance. They asked her and she agreed but without enthusiasm.

Shortly afterwards, Kavita was alone in the living room with her mother. She was listlessly reading a book; her mother, sitting opposite, was sewing gold braid to the green sari that Kavita would wear at the ruby wedding celebrations.

Kavita's attention wandered from the book and she sat, vaguely watching her mother's thin, wrinkled fingers as she plied her needle and thread.

Kavita thought of the two dances she would do at the celebrations. She knew them both well and had practised them the previous day in front of the big mirror in her bedroom. But somehow there was no vivacity, no spirit in her dancing. This was partly the result of her feeling about life at the moment, but it was also the way she felt about her parents' ruby wedding. It was a wonderful opportunity for the Vora children to say thank you for all the love and attention they had received over the years; she knew that was how the others saw it. For Kavita, when she thought back, all her memories except one were of kindness and affection: her parents nursing her when she was ill; the little treats, parties, outings and celebrations; the teaching of dancing – her mother had been her very first teacher before Indu – and all the other, innumerable sacrifices which parents make for their children.

But that one exception still rankled: the time when she was locked in her room. During that day (days? Was it only one day?) when she had wandered lost in the snow, her faith in her parents' love had died. It was still dead. It wouldn't come back. And yet... She looked across at her mother. How old she seemed, old to have so young a daughter, old even for her years. And she was ageing quickly. Inevitably there would come a day when there would be no point in saying, 'I forgive you and thank you for all your love over the years.' They would be beyond all that. Why not forgive and be nice to them now, while there was still time?

'Why did you lock me in my room?' Kavita suddenly asked without the slightest preamble. Strangely, her mother smiled, a smile of relief ebbing its way across her furrowed face.

'Oh, we never thought it would lead to so much trouble – just a little shock, nothing more. We only intended to keep you there for one night and release you next morning. In fact we did but you were already gone. What did we think? Oh Kavita – we were horrified when we realised you had gone off into the snow. But yes, it was an unkind thing, very unkind. Can you forgive us?'

Kavita thought for a moment of all the unkind things she had ever done. She thought of that terrible quarrel when she had screamed at Miles that she could kill him and meant it at the time. For a moment she thought, *If I can find it in my heart to forgive my parents then why not Miles?* But no – she could never forgive Miles.

She pushed that thought away, looked back at her mother and weighed that one unkindness against all the manifestations of her parents' love. 'I forgive you both,' she said, standing up.

Mother and daughter embraced. Then Kavita went straight to her father and said the same thing.

Thereafter her dance practice went better. She entered more joyfully into the other preparations as well – the food, the music, the sending of invitations (so many – all that sticking on of stamps). Yes, Kavita was really looking forward to it now.

THIRTEEN

But a week before the ruby wedding was Janamastami, the celebration of the birth of Krishna. Kavita loved this festival, not quite as much she loved Dwali but almost. And, as they entered the terraced house in Oastler Street that served as the Hindu temple, she felt that old joy, that childish excitement, kindle inside her.

It was there, as they took off their shoes by the door and stowed them away in the big locker; there as they ascended the carpeted stairs; most of all it was there as they entered the big room and looked around. They saw the statuettes lit by the warm lights: Hanuman, the monkey god; Ganesh, the elephant-headed god (god of beginnings); Rama and Sita, eternal male and eternal female; Vishnu, his cobalt-blue body towering above; and of course Krishna himself, the cheeky boy who was also a sage and a god – blue too, but youthfully blue.

Mr Vora went forward, made a money offering and pressed his hands together in a pranam gesture of reverence for the gods. The rest of the family did likewise. Then they sat down on the chadars near the front, more or less in a family group but with Mr Vora and Kamlesh on the male side of the room and Mrs Vora, Kavita, Indu and Lata on the female.

To the right of the room near the stage an oldish woman was chanting, her white hair flowing over a deep-blue sari. As Kavita joined in the responses, it all blended in with a dream of the past that had been in her mind a lot recently: her memory of India; her Indian childhood; the little village – almost a suburb – near Bombay where she had been brought up. Any wish to go back to India had died in her – or so she had thought. But recently there had been murmurings, vague ripples, a wish to start a new life. A feeling that her present existence had reached an impasse.

They joined in the chanting for about an hour. Things were warming up rather slowly and there were still only a few people in the room.

'Let's go downstairs for some tea,' said Mr Vora, leaning towards his wife. He always liked refreshments to help his devotions.

They rose and went down to the long narrow room below. There seemed to be more people here than upstairs, all sitting round tables eating and drinking tea. The Vora family sat down in the remaining vacant chairs at the table immediately inside the door. A tall, sick-looking man approached the table and brought them channas and jhalebi. Then he came back with cups of tea.

They were a mixed company at the table. A local bus driver leant across the table towards Mr Vora. 'You know, I've lived in this town for thirty years and this is my first visit to the temple.'

Mr Vora shrugged. 'And what finally brought you here?'

'Well, I were walking past a few weeks ago and somehow just seeing the temple brought things back, back from when I were a kid in Baroda. Lovely colourful memories. An' I said to myself, at the birth of Krishna I'll go in – revive all them wonderful memories.'

Kavita was listening, interested in this man and his story of childhood memories returning just as hers had come back to her recently. But she was only half listening. The rest of her attention was on an old woman in the hallway painfully taking off her shoes, assisted by a younger man. They turned and Kavita at once recognised Dr Vyas and his mother.

The old woman seemed to have aged since Kavita had last seen her. It was obvious that she was very bad on her feet as she moved towards the tea-room door. Kavita was in a panic as to what she should do. For so long she had shunned Dr Vyas but now courtesy dictated that she should give up her seat to the old woman and there would have to be some polite conversation.

Kavita immediately leapt up and ushered the old woman to her chair, putting her hand under her arm to help her down. Dr Vyas gave Kavita the slightest smile of appreciation from out of his grave, sad eyes.

A cup of tea appeared in front of Mrs Vyas. The bus driver continued with his reminiscences. Mrs Vyas seemed interested and added some comments of her own. 'Yes, I have always felt myself an exile in this England place. I suppose the English have some culture but I've never discovered it.'

'Of course the English have culture,' put in Mr Vora. 'They go to the town hall every Christmas and sing Handel's 'Messiah'.'

'Who was Handel?' asked the bus driver.

'He was a Yorkshireman who lived in the time of Queen Victoria,' said Mr Vora.

Kavita's eyes met those of Dr Vyas in a glance of amusement. 'He was a German who was born in 1685 –

they celebrated his tercentenary last year,' she said. 'Why do you hold forth on subjects you know nothing about? You know that old Mrs Sykes likes Wensleydale and Mr Haigh prefers Red Leicester – that's the level of English culture you should stick to.'

Mr Vora shrugged again. 'Not even Lord Rama himself would have the courage to do battle with the tongue of his own daughter.'

'Let's go back upstairs,' said Mrs Vora, fearing where the discussion would lead.

Upstairs there was still plenty of room. Kavita could have sat anywhere she wanted but she chose to sit beside Mrs Vyas, with Nalin on the other side. Yes, she would think of him as Nalin now, not Dr Vyas. It was time to stop having this cold, formal, sarcastic attitude towards him. And she felt happy.

She said little but she glanced up at Nalin and wondered how she could have been so hostile to this kind, handsome person. And the mother, too. She looked so old – older than Kavita's mother – and so frail. Her conversation with the bus driver had interested Kavita; she had entered into the spirit of it.

And now all the celebrations seemed to be part of some newfound sense of purpose: the smell of the joss sticks; the tinsel reflecting the light from the walls; the gods and goddesses beaming down at them across the room; the sounds of the gongs, the tiny cymbals, the bells, the tablas. All the beauty, all the songs – everything.

The whole evening moved forward in a slow crescendo, which would culminate at midnight at the very moment of Krishna's birth. Right now it was the chanting and singing, the endless telling of the stories about Krishna, the tales of his childhood, his boyhood, his early manhood long, long before he became anything resembling a sage. A young girl in pink, so small, so pretty, was singing a song about Krishna's earliest childhood. She was from the very south of India. Nobody else knew this legend or the song that enshrined it. They joined in tentatively. Then Indu sang and Nalin followed her.

Kavita was surprised. She hadn't expected Nalin to sing but he had a very good voice, really quite beautiful. Kavita had a poor voice but after a while she sang something too – the old familiar song of Krishna and the milkmaids. They all knew this; everyone joined in.

It was getting late and approaching the time when the infant god would be born. Rose petals were passed amongst the women, water splashed across the room. Indu went round with panchamrit and ladled it into cupped hands. For a moment the lights went out and only the candles were left burning in front of the statuesque gods. Kavita experienced the old excitement she had felt at this moment from earliest childhood. Then on went the lights again, bells rang, a gong banged, conch shells sounded out. This was the moment; the baby God had been born into the world. They all moved slowly forward and one by one rocked the tiny cradle.

Nalin rocked it then Kavita touched it gently, rocked it, rocked it tenderly. And she felt as if some infant god really had been born within her somewhere deep inside, a resurgence of happiness, a rainstorm after her long emotional drought.

FOURTEEN

Yvette and Simon had never been to Kavita's home before but they had the instructions written on the back of the ruby wedding invitation: get off at the last mill chimney before Holmefield, go up the steep street on the right, then look for Vora General Stores in a side street on the left.

They found the place – that was no problem – but they felt a bit shy. Not of Kavita, of course; Yvette knew her quite well by now. But there'd be so many other people, complete strangers. They feared they'd be swamped.

Aditi, her hands smeared with strong-smelling spice, greeted them in the hallway. 'Kavita's busy changing for the dancing,' she said breathlessly. 'Just take off your shoes, put them here – that's it – and go into the big room. Sit down anywhere you like.'

They entered, and were quite staggered by the size and beauty of the room. It seemed impossible that such a small-fronted terraced house could contain anything so palatial. But it ran the full length of the house and the family had done it up for the occasion so that it had something of the aura of a fairy castle or an Aladdin's cave: the pictures and batik work round the walls; the rich chadars and cushions on the floor; the exquisite ornaments on the mantelpiece, all lit by soft lighting, candles and side-lamps.

They sat down shyly in a corner. Not many people were there as yet but after about ten minutes an absolute avalanche of friends and relations descended. Blue saris, green saris, red saris, white saris all floated past Yvette's gaze together with numerous dark brown female midriffs, mostly middle aged and bulging somewhat. There were immaculate suits encasing handsome interesting-looking men (Yvette's dream) whilst innumerable bright-eyed toddlers swarmed everywhere like puppies in a dog basket. But despite the crowd, everyone found somewhere to sit and there was even a space at the far end for the entertainers.

Anish, the eldest brother, acted as master of ceremonies whilst Mr and Mrs Vora sat to one side as if overwhelmed by everything. Anish made his rather formal speech, congratulating his parents, thanking them for all their devotion over the years. Applause. Then there was music, some slides and a bit of singing. But the thing that Yvette had been waiting for came at the end of the entertainment: Kavita' s dancing.

How lovely Kavita looked – the parrot-green sari wrapped round her beautiful slim body; the *bangadi* on her dark arms, a kamarband round her narrow waist, janjers jingling around her small ankles.

She came to the front of the clear space, stood for a moment then made a namaste gesture to the audience. 'Friends,' she began. 'I want to dedicate these two dances to my dear parents.'

She went on to describe the dances but Yvette's thoughts were elsewhere. It was that word 'dear' which had struck her. Yvette was really very fond of her father and of course Clare, she loved her as well. But she wouldn't have used the word 'dear' to describe them.

No, there was something significant about the sincerity that Kavita had put into that phrase 'my dear parents'.

Kavita's behaviour later in the evening puzzled Yvette. As the only person who Yvette really knew, she had expected Kavita to make a big fuss of her. But no, she and Simon hardly saw her and had to introduce themselves and start up conversations with complete strangers.

Yvette's puzzlement became even greater later on when she went through to the kitchen for some food. Yvette, not knowing which was the kitchen door, opened the wrong one. This led into the only other room on the ground floor. She glanced in and realised her mistake but in that glance she had seen Kavita and Dr Vyas alone together in close conversation.

'Sorry,' Yvette muttered and withdrew.

Kavita and Dr Vyas alone together? Yvette remembered that strange snowy evening only a year and a half ago. Then Kavita had been running away from home, from her parents, from any contact with Dr Vyas. Yet here she was referring to her 'dear' parents and conversing alone – and closely – with Dr Vyas. What did it all mean?

Her suppositions came together at the very end of the evening, or rather the early morning, for the party went on late. Despite the initial isolation, Yvette and Simon had enjoyed themselves but by two a.m. felt it was late enough. They had put on their coats and were about to go into the kitchen to say goodbye to Mr and Mrs Vora. But Kavita was in there as well with Dr Vyas.

Intuitively Yvette drew back into the shadows of the hallway. She tried not to overhear the conversation but could not help it. One sentence explained everything when Kavita said in a somewhat faltering voice, 'Mummy, Daddy – I've agreed to marry Dr Vyas.'

FIFTEEN

Mrs Vyas looked up at that picture that she loved so much. It was India, the India of long ago, of flickering memory. A village stood somewhere to the right with women going about their evening task of drawing water from the well. Beyond, the sun was setting, not one of those lingering English sunsets but the sunset of India where it seemed to hover for only a few moments, a great ruby of light, before dropping to darkness.

'Every time I look at that picture I want to go home ' she said with a sigh.

Nalin had heard it all before; it was a constant moan that in the past had greatly irritated him. But tonight the refrain was more welcome. Just a little earlier that evening he had read an advert for a job back in Bombay which attracted him; the pay was good, the post prestigious. Back in the past, when he had been in India, the thought of being in England as a qualified doctor had seemed very glamorous. Yet now he was here what was he after all? Just another Indian doctor. Why, at that party at the Voras almost every man present had been a doctor except Mr Vora himself.

But supposing he went back to India? It would be different now because he himself would have changed. He was no longer the impoverished student; instead, he would be qualified, with money and a beautiful young wife. Yes — Kavita. And he pictured himself introducing her to his relations and friends and she stretching her beautiful slim arm from beneath her sari to clasp their hands.

'This is my wife Kavita,' he would say. Yes, it was worth thinking about.

And so he indulged his mother a bit and entered into her feelings about the painting. It was a fine painting, in any case, painted by an Indian artist who had spent the last twenty years of his life in Holmefield; Nalin had known him slightly. The artist had died in early middle age with a slight reputation, scarcely what he deserved. All his paintings had that somewhat mournful look: a vision of India, but not quite the actuality, seen through an ache of exile. Yes, one shouldn't spend all one's life as an exile. It was a mistake, definitely a mistake.

SIXTEEN

Yvette hadn't seen Kavita for a long time, not since that ruby wedding party. That was three months ago, back in November, and now it was February. And then she met her – no, it wasn't really a meeting.

The market arcade, mid-morning, lots of shoppers around. Yvette saw Kavita coming towards her from about ten yards away and prepared to greet her warmly. But then she noticed the expression on Kavita's face, a strange look of self-absorbed despair. Yvette's greeting froze and Kavita walked past without recognising her.

For Miles that winter seemed the longest he had ever known. The snow appeared to linger forever, nestling against the pinnacles of the old Minster, crenellating the city walls and flooding the great flatness of the surrounding fields with white.

For himself, everything was whiteness as well – whiteness or blankness. He mixed little with other people, painted little, and his teachers despaired of seeing his early promise go anywhere. Then in early March something happened that ever afterwards he looked back on and wondered, 'Did it happen? Was it a dream? Was it a nightmare?'

It was an afternoon of exceptional dreariness. The snow lay scattered over every rooftop and the sky was uniformly grey; it was impossible to believe that there was a sun somewhere, anywhere.

Miles was alone in his flat, which occupied the top floor of a four-storey block. He flicked listlessly through the pages of an art history book they were supposed to be studying, wondering how he would fill the blankness of the afternoon, of the evening.

A ring on his doorbell. He went downstairs. Kavita! He couldn't take it in. There she stood, casually dressed in jeans, T-shirt, a somewhat tatty overcoat open at the front.

He looked at her. Neither spoke. She walked in. He closed the door and only then did she come close to him, put her arms around him, lay her head on his shoulder.

'1 had to come to you,' she murmured. 'Don't ask me anything. Don't ask me to explain. I – I – just had to come.'

They stood there embracing for a long time. Then they heard the footsteps of one of the other occupants. 'Come upstairs,' Miles said.

They went up. Miles felt ashamed of the filthy state he had allowed the flat to get into. He brewed some tea. He couldn't believe that Kavita was there with him. The mood of ten minutes ago seemed ancient history. But what did it mean? What had she come to tell him? How was she? He glanced in her face. Was she happy? Was she sad? Only an enigmatic half-smile answered him. No: he was totally bewildered.

They sipped their tea in silence to begin with. Miles' hand trembled; he could hardly hold the cup. Eventually he began to ask her things, specific questions, but he got nowhere. Half-exasperated, he stood up. 'But – I mean, you had a motive for coming here. What do you want?'

'It's a matter of what you want. Whatever you want, I will give it to you.'

For a moment the old Kavita came into her face, that smile, not the mischievous one but the loving one. She stood up and flung herself tightly against him. After the long months of frustration, Miles found her intensely arousing. He wanted her, not next year or even tomorrow, but now. He forced his fingers down the back of her waistband, tugged at her shirt, reached down greedily for the soft naked flesh of her hips. The popper of her jeans burst open and he pushed her backwards onto to the bed. She neither helped him nor resisted but lay there, letting him do whatever he wanted.

Hastily he tore off her clothes. And then, when they were both naked, he hurled himself at her with a violence and desperation that was quite out of character. There was no tenderness, none whatever. It was as if she were a ghost, a phantom, and this apparent reality of beautiful soft flesh would suddenly vanish if he didn't enjoy it at once.

Was he happy? Was he sad? He didn't know. He seemed to be in a strange state where bliss and agony merged.

And when it was over, he looked into Kavita's eyes. He hoped that that lovely look of love and tenderness would be back there again in her dark pupils. But it wasn't. There was only blankness, nothingness.

And he felt in himself a terrible emptiness.

*

They got up and dressed. Still Kavita hardly spoke. Miles didn't know what to say. Eventually he asked, 'Shall we go out for a meal? Or perhaps I could cook something for you here?'

'No. I have a train at five twenty. What is it now?'

'Quarter to five.'

'I'll have to be quick.'

'I'll see you to the station.'

'No, don't. Let's part here.'

They went down to the hall.

'Well – when do I see you again?'

'I'll contact you.'

'But when?'

'Don't fret. All will be well in the end if the gods are willing.'

They kissed. Then she opened the door and went off down the snowy street.

SEVENTEEN

Time passed – hours, days, weeks – and Miles heard nothing. What was going on? Did that afternoon really happen?

It was May now and he could stand it no longer. One evening he went down to the call box armed with four ten-pence pieces. Trembling, he dialled the code for Holmefield, dialled her number. But he got Mr Vora. His answers seemed evasive. 'Aditi is in the shop. She can explain better than me. I will fetch her.'

Miles waited with intense impatience.

'Yes – she is busy I'm afraid,' Mr Vora said eventually.

'But it's Kavita I want to speak to.'

'Well—'

The line went dead. Miles didn't bother with another ten pence. Instead, next day he went over to Holmefield. He reached the Voras' house in the early evening. Kamlesh opened the door and immediately Miles saw a particular look come across his face, a look of pain, embarrassment and yet of warm friendship. For a moment Miles remembered that time long ago when Kamlesh had asked him to paint the scenery. Now Kamlesh clasped Miles' hand in both of his in a gesture that was almost an embrace.

'You have come to see Kavita?'

'Yes.'

'She isn't here. She left a letter with me for you in case you ever came seeking her. I'll fetch it.'

Miles felt an icy pain beneath his forehead. He knew that something terrible had happened or was going to happen. Whatever that letter contained, it was not good news. And yet he was anxious to have it, to read an explanation in her own hand.

Kamlesh came downstairs and handed him the letter. 'Would you like to sit down and read it here?'

'No – I'll take it away with me.'

He turned to go and for a moment Kamlesh placed his hand on Miles' shoulder.

*

Miles reached a small park, sat down on a bench and read the letter in the fading daylight.

My dearest, dearest Miles,

I would do anything to spare you this pain but things cannot be otherwise than as they are and I am leaving this letter with Kamlesh in case you ever come looking for me. By the time that you read it (if you read it) I will be in India. I've agreed to marry Dr Vyas and he has been appointed to a post in Bombay. His mother always wanted to go back to India and this is how things have worked out. Indu and her three children are going to India with us for a holiday.

I shall be marrying Dr Vyas in a small village near Bombay on May 15th. Don't ask me to explain that afternoon in York. I can't explain anything. As I write this, my mind is in a whirlpool (see my awful handwriting). I can't make sense of anything, least of all my own emotions. I have tried so hard to please everyone – you, my parents, Dr Vyas. Perhaps I shall end up by pleasing no one, not even myself.

Don't grieve for me when I am gone. Look to your own life and to what your talents will achieve in future years.

Don't spend all your time regretting what is lost. Promise.

Don't try to contact me ever again. But be certain that I really mean this little word with which I end this letter—

Love, Kavita

END OF PART TWO

PART THREE

ONE

The jumbo jet started sinking downwards. Kavita clutched at Indu. Lata, Malti and Kishore were excited, scrambling to look out of the window as the hills of Bombay appeared below. But Kavita was trembling.

'What are you frightened of?' Indu asked, putting a sisterly arm around her shoulder. 'It is just that big hill over there – Pali Hill they call it. There was a bad crash some years ago. The planes from Europe have to fly over it and then abruptly down. That's why it feels so bad.'

'Oh it's not the aeroplane landing I'm frightened of. It's – it's—'

'Kavita – Kavita – what is the matter with you? Nalin will be meeting us at the airport. You should be excited. Think: when you last saw Bombay you were a tiny little girl. Now you're a woman and about to be married.'

But Kavita put her arms around her sister and clung to her desperately. They were sinking, sinking, sinking…

TWO

It was one of those early summer evenings when the incessant song of the curlews on the high moors seemed to fill the whole dusk with a strange weariness. Yvette was in the living room. She would have liked to be in the downstairs bedroom, which was the great focus of attention. But no, she had to be content with the living room and try to imagine what was going on beyond that wall.

Clare was in labour. Everything was going smoothly. Randal was with her and a nurse had just arrived, a plumpish girl with fluffy blonde hair and a sunburnt face; she seemed to inspire confidence. Yvette had been asked to fill a hot-water bottle. That had slightly puzzled her.

'It's for the baby,' her father explained.

The baby – of course, the baby. At the end of all this there would be a baby in the house. It was exciting. Yvette was so used to being an only child, had been for sixteen years now, that the idea that she would ever have a half-sister or -brother had never occurred to her. But here it was; it was actually happening. There would be a big age gap; she would almost feel like a mother for this baby. It was odd.

Randal seemed to have been especially kind to her recently, as if anxious not to let her feel left out. Clare too. Yvette had forgiven Clare for the occasional bossiness of the early days of the marriage. Yes, she felt she must love Clare and something of the feeling of long ago had come back to her. But right now there seemed very little that Yvette could do except wait.

Would it be a long wait? For no particular reason Yvette thought it would be. What could she do? She thought of looking at one of her poetry books but she was too excited. Instead she just looked out of the window, a favourite occupation. The sun had set beyond the solitary sycamore but there was still plenty of light. Yvette stayed there, sitting on the sill and watching the full moon getting brighter high above the moorland, and the sheep and lambs nibbling the grass in the intake fields.

A sudden cry startled her. Where did it come from? The moors? No. It was from the next room. Was it Clare? Was she in pain? No, of course not. It was the baby.

THREE

Indu sat alone on the terrace, her head on her arms, her whole body shaking. Occasionally she looked up at the swiftly falling sun but mostly her eyes were closed, somehow too pained for tears. She had shut the children up in their room like caged animals. They had clamoured to know what was wrong, what had happened. Where was their auntie? But no. Even at this time of stress and panic she had to remember that she was a mother and to protect her children somehow from the terrible things that had happened.

Her mind passed swiftly through the events of the day but always reached the same point and recoiled in horror. In the early morning everything had seemed to be fine. True, Kavita appeared a bit strange, subdued. But she had been a bit strange for some while. Pre-marital jitters, nothing more. Lots of people got them.

They had gone to the temple to pray, Kavita all in her finery but with her eyes cast down, sad somehow. Lord Ganesh, the God of Beginnings; he had been worshipped. Had they done something wrong? He had been offered the coconut as usual, everything according to form.

They moved on to the big hall where the wedding itself would take place. So many people. And then Kavita had gone alone to a separate small room to have her sacred bath and to put on the wedding sari, the special one, white with red braid. And – oh God, could Indu ever get over that moment?

Kavita took a long time, so long. Eventually Indu had grown impatient, gone towards the room. It was that first thing she saw – the trickle of blood under the door. How could she ever forget it, even if she lived for a million years? And then, throwing open the door. Kavita on the floor, the white sari untouched except by a bloodstain. The knife. How did she get the knife, the long sharp one – how did she conceal it? But did it matter how she did it? Why she did it? It was in the past. No matter that it happened this very morning, it was past, over. Nothing that was ever done could bring it back. Like the battle of Kurukshetra or the massacre at Amritsar, it was over, finished, irredeemable.

And Indu thought of the people she would have to tell. For a moment she saw the prematurely aged faces of her parents. Oh my God. Oh Kavita – why did you do it? Why did you do something so horrible? We loved you – we all loved you. If you had been my daughter instead of my sister I couldn't have loved you more. Oh Kavita. Kavita.

For a moment Indu lifted her eyes. The sun was almost at the horizon. Down below two men were leading a water buffalo to a shallow pond to be washed; some women were returning from the well with their filled pitchers; the koyal birds were singing in the mango trees.

And the sun sank down into the darkness.

Another day was ended.

FOUR

Miles sat in the living room at Randal and Clare's. He had heard the news from India and knew that only Clare could comfort him.

Randal and Yvette were out. The new baby, Arthur, only three weeks old, was asleep. Miles talked to Clare for hours, so it seemed. In a way her answers were platitudes, the usual thoughts about time healing all things. What more was there to say? And ultimately it was true – in the end, in the very end.

Eventually Arthur stirred and cried. Clare got up, fetched him from the cradle, comforted him for a while. Then she undid her dress and put the tiny head to her breast. Clare's words, merely as words, hadn't helped Miles but her presence – that was different. He looked across at her now, the long fair hair drooping to her blue-skirted lap; the eyes shielded by the lids as she looked downwards; the baby's tiny head edged against the softness of her breast. Really, if he admitted it, this was what life was all about for a man: eternal womanhood, Madonna and child. Or rather mother and child. That was enough; there was no need for angels.

And if it wasn't about this, what was it about?

Was it about anything?

END OF PART THREE

POSTLUDE

But that was well-nigh twenty years ago. This was the present and in a sense all that mattered. The actuality – the children playing in the sunlit street and the houses, the mills and the moors beyond. And what had happened in those twenty years for Miles? A growing reputation. It wasn't quite the great fame he had sometimes dreamt of but neither was it the utter failure he had often feared. But then the main thing in those years had really been Clare.

Randal had died in late middle age and a few years afterwards Miles had married her. She wasn't quite the slim, beautiful girl he had once known but she was herself; she was Clare and all the emotions he had ever felt seemed to be focused in their relationship. If he could have any part of his life over again it would be those last few years. Not the years of youth; they were too painful.

He glanced up and saw that the Indian girl in the purple sari had returned. Good. She was standing by that shop, looking at something in the window. Frantically Miles squeezed some purple acrylic on to his palette and started to paint.

Yes, the intense years.

Kavita.

*

And worlds still pirouette their stars,
whilst on that stage fresh actors meet,
dim picture in a golden frame –
bright sari in a darkened street.

ACKNOWLEDGEMENTS

This novel has been published posthumously and therefore my ability to acknowledge the relevant people who assisted Ian in any way in its writing and research is somewhat limited. In the chapter heading 'Bright Sari in a Darkened Street' of his semi-autobiographical work Yorkshire Lives and Landscapes, Ian detailed his experiences of attending cultural events at the Huddersfield Hindu Temple in Zetland Street. I know how much he appreciated the help, support and kind invitations extended to him at that time by the Mehta family and others in the Hindu community, and I must acknowledge those important contributions.

My own thanks are due to Isobel Stirk and Brian Endley for reading through the original typescript, highlighting its merits and encouraging me to pursue its publication. I will always be indebted to SOBS and the many kind friends who have supported me through very difficult times since the loss of Ian, either by valuable practical and emotional help or simply by keeping in touch by telephone, letter or e-mail. I refrain from naming people individually for fear of omitting anyone by mistake but you all know who you are. My thanks are heartfelt and sincere.

I am also grateful and fortunate in engaging the services and help of all at 2QT Ltd, publishers of Settle, for their sympathetic editing, proofreading and design work. My especial thanks are due to Karen Holmes for ensuring that Ian's unique 'voice' has been fully retained throughout its stages to publication. My greatest praise for the finished work can only be to say that Ian would have been very happy with the outcome.

Catherine Emberson

Ian M. Emberson

ABOUT THE AUTHOR

Ian M. Emberson was born in 1936 at Hove in Sussex and was proud to have been christened by the poet Andrew Young. His mother was a gardener's daughter who had been brought up in the village of Alloway in Ayrshire where Robert Burns was born. His father was a journalist from Essex. Ian took to painting and writing in early childhood and pursued these activities all his life.

During his National Service, he was in the Royal Signals and served in Cyprus 1955–57. He went on to earn a living in both horticulture and librarianship in different parts of the country, settling in Thurstonland in Huddersfield in 1971 after obtaining the post of Music Librarian at the Central Library. In his Dalesman article about Ian, the broadcaster Ian McMillan tells how Ian encouraged both himself, and other young writers such as Simon Armitage, when he organised many poetry events in Huddersfield in the 1970s as Secretary of Kirklees Arts Council at a time when the Huddersfield poetry scene was taking off.

Ian took early retirement in 1986 in order to concentrate on painting and writing. His work as an artist is best known through postcards and book illustrations. His publications include six books of poems and two of prose-poems, as well as many journal and magazine articles. In 1996, Bradford Playhouse produced his play Cockerel Crowing Dawn based on the life of the Russian composer Mussorgsky. He also wrote the libretto for Daniel Bath's opera The Forest, first performed at the Hebden Bridge Festival in June 2003. Five other composers have set his poetry to music: Peter Copley; John Bartlett; Gordon Dyson; Robin Terry, and Katharine Petkovski.

Ian met his wife, Catherine, through the Brontë Society in 1988 and they later married and lived in Todmorden. Together they worked on various pieces of research. One of these led to the discovery of the Reverend George Sowden's Recollections of the Brontës, which had lain virtually forgotten for more than one hundred years. This was published in May 2005. In November of the same year, the Brontë Society published Ian's book Pilgrims from Loneliness: an interpretation of Charlotte Brontë's Jane Eyre and Villette.

Yorkshire Lives and Landscapes, published by Sutton in 2006, was a semi-autobiographical view of Yorkshire as seen through the eyes of a 'comer-in' and featured the county's cultural traditions, the experience of walking the Pennine Way and life in a small village, amongst other subjects.

Sunrise at Cyprus: Caroline's Mediterranean Journal, an e-book, was Ian's last published work. He died unexpectedly in 2013.

Ian was a polymath and his creative oeuvre is considerable, with many unpublished poems, essays, plays and art work still to see the light of day. Bright Sari in a Darkened Street represents the first steps in the posthumous promotion of Ian's legacy. He was a kind, generous and highly sensitive man and his creative spirit was unique. He is deeply mourned by all who knew and loved him, but his work will live on and continue to attract acclaim.

BY THE SAME AUTHOR

Poetry

Doodles in the Margins of My Life

Swallows Return

Mourning Ring: poems about the Brontës

Pirouette of Earth: a Novel in Verse

Natural Light

Messages from Distant Shores

Prose Poems

The Comet of 1811

The Snake and the Star

Fiction

Sunrise at Cyprus: Caroline's Mediterranean Journal

Non-Fiction

Pilgrims from Loneliness: an interpretation of Charlotte Brontë's Jane Eyre and Villette

Yorkshire Lives and Landscapes

Details of these publication are available from the website: www.ianemberson.co.uk

Printed in July 2019
by Rotomail Italia S.p.A., Vignate (MI) - Italy